RED CAVALRY

A Critical Companion

RED CAVALRY

A Critical Companion

Edited by Charles Rougle

Northwestern University Press

The American Association of Teachers

of Slavic and East European Languages

Northwestern University Press

Evanston, Illinois 60208-4210

Copyright © 1996 by Northwestern University Press

Printed in the United States of America

ISBN 0-8101-1213-2

Library of Congress Cataloging-in-Publication Data

Red Cavalry : a critical companion / edited by Charles Rougle.

    p. cm. — (Northwestern/AATSEEL critical companions to

Russian literature)

  Includes bibliographical references.

  ISBN 0-8101-1213-2 (alk. paper)

  1. Babel', I. (Isaak), 1894–1941. Konarmiia. I. Rougle,

Charles, 1946–   . II. Series.

PG3476.B2K636   1996

891.73'42—dc20   96-8498

                                       CIP

Contents

Acknowledgments

Some of the material in this volume has been previously published in somewhat different form and appears here by permission: Carol Luplow, "Paradox and the Search for Value in Babel's *Red Cavalry*," *Slavic and East European Journal* 23, no. 2 (1979): 216–32, reprinted by permission of *Slavic and East European Journal*; Milton Ehre, "Babel's *Red Cavalry*: Epic and Pathos, Culture and History," Slavic Review 40, no. 2 (June 1981): 228–40, reprinted by permission of the American Association for the Advancement of Slavic Studies; Victor Terras, "Line and Color: The Structure of I. Babel's Short Stories in *Red Cavalry*," *Studies in Short Fiction* 3 (1966): 141–56, copyright © 1966 by Newberry College, reprinted by permission of *Studies in Short Fiction*; excerpts from Isaac Babel, *1920 Diary*, translated by H. T. Willetts, edited and with an introduction by Carol J. Avins (New Haven, Conn.: Yale University Press, 1995), reprinted by permission of Yale University Press.

NOTE ON TRANSLITERATION

For ease of reading, the "y" system of transliteration (Thomas Shaw's System I) has been used in the text. In the bibliography the "i" system, or Shaw's System II, has been chosen for its greater accuracy and is used except in Russian words occurring in the titles of works by authors using another system.

NOTE ON NAMES

Three cultures and nations—Russia, Ukraine, and Poland—meet and mix in the geographical area in which *Red Cavalry* is set. Many cities, towns, and villages, therefore, have two or more variants. The transliterated Russian spellings in the text below are in no way meant to imply that these places are somehow more Russian than Ukrainian or Polish, but they are for obvious reasons the ones Babel used, and they are generally also the variants chosen in the best known English translation of the work. The recent McDuff translation, in contrast, prefers the Polish variants of the place names below.

Russian	Polish
Berestechko	Beresteczko
Chesniki	Cześniki
Leshniuv	Leszniów
Lvov	Lwów
Zamoste	Zamość
Zbruch	Zbrucz

The reader will also note some differences in the names of characters in the book. Morison speaks of "Sandy" the Christ and "Matthew" Pavlichenko and "Andie" Vosmiletov, but other translators and commentators prefer the more Russian names "Sashka," "Matvey," and "Andryushka."

I ❄ INTRODUCTION

KOVEL

ZAMOSTE
CHESNIKI

SOKAL

POLAND

Bug

DUBNO

BERESTECHKO
KOZIN   VERBA

BRODY

BUSK

LVOV

G A L I C I A

Zbruch

HUNGARY

0   50   100 miles

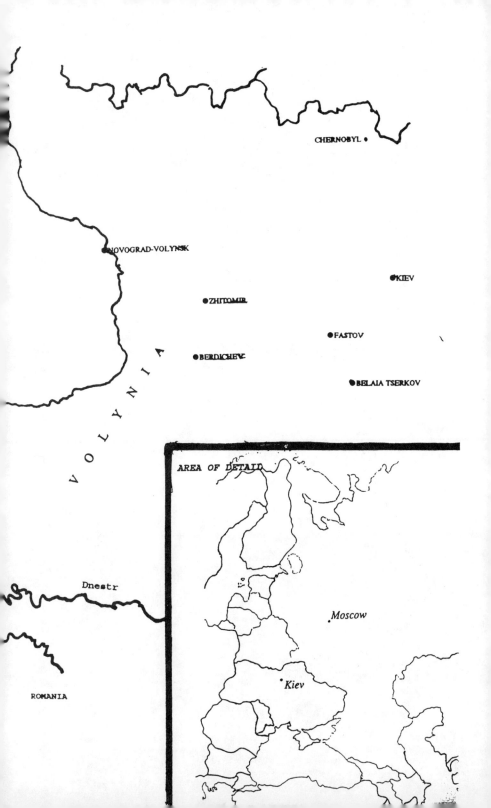

CHERNOBYL •

• NOVOGRAD-VOLYNSK

• KIEV

• ZHITOMIR

• FASTOV

• BERDICHEV

• BELAIA TSERKOV

V O L Y N I A

AREA OF DETAIL

Dnestr

Moscow

Kiev

ROMANIA

Isaac Babel and His Odyssey of War and Revolution

CHARLES ROUGLE

Biographical Sketch

Red Cavalry is the masterpiece of Isaak Emmanuilovich Babel, one of Russia's greatest short story writers. Greeted as a major literary event when its first thirty-four stories appeared in scattered newspapers and journals in 1923–25, the 1926 book edition went through numerous reprintings in the following decade only to be subjected to a prolonged period of forced neglect – Babel was arrested for unspecified crimes in the Stalinist purges of 1939 and executed. Since his rehabilitation in the 1960s he is once again attracting the serious attention of readers and critics in Russia; the body of Western scholarship also has become quite extensive, especially considering that the entire oeuvre of this notoriously meticulous craftsman could easily be accommodated by two or at most three moderately sized volumes.[1]

One might think that the biography of a writer of such undisputed stature would by this time be familiar in great detail. It is not. What we do know has come to us from the brief memoirs of his daughter and his second wife and from a variety of mostly anecdotal and not entirely reliable sources.[2] Although recent archival research has added some facts and corrected others,[3] large gaps remain. We do not know for certain exactly what Babel was doing during significant periods of his life, nor do we have many nonfictional statements on his interpretation of many important events and phenomena. He remains something of a puzzle, and he himself contributed to the confusion with ambivalent or misleading biographical information. To begin with the details that are certain, Babel was born on 30 June 1894 in the Black Sea port of Odessa and grew up there and in the nearby town of Nikolaev. His father was a moderately successful Jewish merchant who first sold agricultural machinery and then owned a small warehouse. On the surface, at least, it might have seemed that Isaak would follow in his father's footsteps. He entered the Nicholas I Commercial School in 1906, where besides studying business-related subjects he acquired a fluent command of French and a love of French literature. Barred by the Jewish quota from entering the university, upon graduation in 1911 he went on to the Kiev Institute of Finance and Business, moving with it in 1915 when it was evacuated to Saratov and receiving a degree in economics there in the spring of 1916.[4] This completed his formal education. Although he enrolled in the Law School of the Petersburg Neurological Institute in the fall of 1916, he seems to have spent little effort on his studies and instead was by this time committed to becoming a writer.

Already at this early point the facts of Babel's life begin to blur. He devotes a full third of his 1924 "Autobiography" to this period. There he claims to have arrived in Petersburg in 1915 and for a full year to have lived a poverty-stricken Bohemian existence in a cellar rented from a drunken waiter, hiding from the police because he lacked a residence permit (required for Jews), and unsuccessfully hawking his stories in various editorial offices. Until, that is, he met Maksim Gorky, who discovered his talent and published his first stories and then sent the callow youth out into "the world" to get to know life and discipline his craft.[5]

The only problem with this account is that most of it contradicts independently established facts. Babel was actually living legally and relatively comfortably in Petersburg. He may not even have come to the city until 1916, which means that his success was much more rapid than he claims.[6] The reasons for these distortions may be quasi-literary, for the image of the estranged outsider is central to much of Babel's frankly autobiographical fiction, and he is not the first writer to impose his literary persona on his real self. Or perhaps he needed a set of fictionalized facts to protect a private sphere for himself. We may never know for sure.

At any rate, the winter of 1916 does mark the real beginning of Babel's career as a writer, and whether Gorky "sent" him into the world or he went on his own, it was into the world he went, gathering experiences and honing the keen powers of observation for which he is deservedly famous. The spring and summer of 1917, one of the most turbulent periods in Russia's history, are another blank spot in his biography. In October he enlisted in the army and was sent to the Romanian front. He has left no record, fictional or otherwise, of this experience, although indirectly his treatment of war themes may owe much to impressions formed during these months.[7] He was not there long, as he soon fell ill with malaria and was demobilized by early 1918. There is some uncertainty as to his activities in this period as well. In his "Autobiography" he notes that he worked for the Cheka, the Bolshevik security police, and in 1930 he dates his service to October (Old Style) 1917.[8] His daughter Nathalie dismisses the entire account as fiction.[9] The complete facts may never surface, but the circumstantial evidence tends to support at least part of Babel's claim. He spoke of writing a novel about the Cheka, and he also claims that Russian émigrés later shunned him in Paris for his rumored involvement.[10] It is not unreasonable to assume, as others have done, that he worked with interrogations or translations,[11] although it is highly unlikely that he did so before returning to Russia in 1918.

This chronology is in itself interesting, because it means that at the same time Babel was working for the Bolsheviks, he was also supporting some of their most vocal critics. Throughout the spring of 1918, his principal writing activity consisted of a series of sketches of Petersburg life published in Gorky's anti-Bolshevik newspaper *New Life*, which Lenin closed down in July. For understandable reasons, Babel ignores or glosses over this period in his later autobiographical statements, but his dual involvement is actually not as hypocritical as it may seem at first glance. Although the Cheka had a good deal on its conscience from the very beginning, it had yet to launch the full-scale terror that accompanied the outbreak of the civil war. Also, the ideological lines between the Bolsheviks and their left-of-center critics still displayed a certain porosity, and there were many cases – Gorky himself is one – of limited cooperation between them, especially if the only alternative seemed to be counterrevolution. Nor, at this early stage, had the incompatibility of revolutionary and humanist ideals become fully obvious to all. The evolution of Babel's views is impossible to assess exactly, but whatever doubts he may have had (and there is some evidence of hesitation in the *New Life* sketches), they did not prevent him from continuing in the service of the revolution. In the summer of 1918 he participated in a grain-requisitioning expedition to the Volga region, an enterprise that more often than not was met by the rural populace with hostility and violence. Like many other intellectuals, that fall and winter he worked for the Commissariat of Enlightenment (Narkompros); at one point, at least, he was involved with one of its many adult education projects. Most of 1919 is another blank until the fall, when we find him again in uniform, this time defending Petersburg against the White Army forces of General Yudenich. The major event of his personal life in that year was his marriage to Evgeniya Gronfein, whom he had known since his student days in Kiev.

Although Babel undoubtedly saw a great deal during these two years, he had not yet plunged into the thick of things, for he had caught only fleeting glimpses of the civil war raging throughout the country. The need for firsthand experience was most certainly what persuaded him in the spring of 1920 to apply to the southern division of the Russian Telegraph Agency (YUGROSTA) for service as a war correspondent with the Cossacks of Semen Budyonny's First Cavalry, which had just been sent into battle to drive the Poles out of present-day Ukraine. Again there is some confusion as to the exact chronology of Babel's service. One critic states that he joined the unit on 24 May 1920, but no evidence is offered in support of this.[12] Many observers have uncritically accepted 3 June, the date of the first entry in the diary he kept throughout the campaign, but this probably should read 3 July instead.[13]

Whenever Babel joined Budyonny, he remained with the Cossacks as a correspondent for the newspaper *The Red Cavalryman* until the early fall, at which time the First Cavalry was transferred to the southern front against the disintegrating White Army forces of General Wrangel. He returned to Odessa and spent the next three years there and in the Caucasus with his wife, moving on to Moscow in late 1923. It was during this period, by far the most productive in his life, that the two cycles on which his literary fame largely rests were drafted or completed. By September 1924, the four so-called Odessa tales and all but a few of the *Red Cavalry* stories had appeared in Moscow and Odessa periodicals, principally the avant-gardist *Lef*, Aleksandr Voronsky's *Red Virgin Soil* (the best literary journal of the day), and the newspaper of the Odessa regional party executive committee. Little known until now outside Odessa and the Russian literary elite of the capitals, Babel became a national figure overnight. "Babel is creating an uproar in Moscow," Konstantin Fedin wrote to Gorky. "Everyone is ecstatic about him."[14] Especially *Red Cavalry* was received by many of his contemporaries as a harbinger of the new Soviet literature; here was a work of extremely high artistic quality that was written moreover by an author almost unknown before the revolution, and about the events that already had become central to the Soviet myth of genesis. Contributing further to Babel's fame were the Odessa stories that appeared at about the same time. Lusty, exuberant tales of passion and violence set in the colorful Jewish underworld of Odessa, they are a stylistic tour de force of a mature master. Babel's place in the contemporary pantheon was assured, bringing with it the usual privileges: a good income, a comfortable apartment, a summer home, opportunities for foreign travel. Unfortunately, however, it also catapulted him into the middle of an inflamed ideological debate that would ultimately have disastrous consequences for participants on all sides. Babel epitomized the so-called fellow travelers – writers who did not oppose the revolution, but who were nonproletarian in social origin and non-Marxist in ideological outlook. The party initially looked upon these artists and their unofficial journal *Red Virgin Soil* with considerable tolerance, but from the very beginning there was an organized assault on the fellow travelers by more doctrinaire leftist critics and literary bureaucrats, who viewed them with suspicion and resentment.

Red Cavalry landed squarely in the middle of this struggle for literary hegemony. The controversy over Babel erupted in March 1924 with an angry denunciation by none other than General Semen Budyonny. In an article in the militant proletarian journal *October*, Budyonny accused him of ignorance, cowardice, and willful slander of the glorious First Cavalry. In actual fact, he was probably to be regarded as a counterrevolutionary:

> The old, rotten, degenerate intelligentsia is filthy and depraved. Its brilliant representatives . . . found themselves on the other side of the barricade, but here is Babel, who has remained here out of cowardice or due to circumstances, telling us a lot of old gibberish refracted through the prism of his sadism and degeneracy.[15]

Budyonny's article initiated a three-year-long debate on Babel. Many of the best critics of the day defended his portrayal of the revolution as truthful and praised his courageous and honest approach to the subject. Detractors reiterated and varied Budyonny's main points, albeit usually in less crude and florid language. Although even many of these were willing to acknowledge Babel's artistic talent, they objected to his "naturalism," by which was meant both a surfeit of physiological and especially erotic detail and a tendency to view the revolution not as a necessary and inevitable historical process consistent with Marxist-Leninist principles, but as a chaotic, elemental, almost biological force beyond the control or even understanding of its movers, who were depicted as savages and bandits.

If political events in the Soviet Union had followed a more evolutionary course, Babel might well have emerged on top of the dispute. As evidenced by journal and newspaper articles and a collection of studies published in 1928,[16] attention was gradually focusing more on the aesthetic, as opposed to the ideological, side of his work. The days for such concerns in literature were numbered, however, and Babel was among the first to feel the harsh change in climate that followed upon the official decision in December 1927 to abandon the relatively liberal New Economic Policy and launch the Soviet Union on the First Five-Year Plan. Forced industrialization and collectivization brought with them increasingly militant demands for ideological commitment and conformity, and it was not long before fellow traveler writers were once again defending themselves against charges of counterrevolution. Budyonny obliged once again on 26 October 1928, this time in an open letter to Maksim Gorky. The attack added nothing new to the earlier charges, but in the harsher political climate of the day it was much more ominous. Gorky came to Babel's defense with praise for *Red Cavalry* and a plea for tolerance and respect,[17] but it is difficult to say what turn this battle might have taken had not Stalin himself intervened on Gorky's urging and pronounced the book "not as bad as all that."[18]

A great deal of damage, however, had already been done. Babel suffered emotionally from the poisoned atmosphere the controversy had created. He referred to these years as the "horrible Moscow period" of his life and lamented the "sickening professional environment devoid of art or creative freedom" in which he was forced to work.[19] These disruptive pressures, combined with fragile health and mounting personal problems, had an inhibiting effect on the volume of his literary production, which was never prolific under the best of circumstances. His marriage was breaking up in 1926, by which time his wife, mother, and sister had emigrated to Europe, settling in Belgium and then France. He visited them there in 1927–28 and again in 1932–33 and 1935, but the rift remained permanent. The income from his earlier work was generous but insufficient, and he turned to screenplays to supplement it.[20] His remaining production was slight, consisting of a handful of stories (some of them, however, among the best he ever wrote) and two plays, one unsuccessful (*Sunset*, 1928) and the other repressed (*Mariya*, 1935).

During all this, the "sickening professional environment" in the Soviet Union did not improve – quite the contrary – and Stalin's reported intervention provided only a partial and temporary respite. Babel returned in September 1933 from his second trip abroad to find "all sorts of absurd but sinister rumors" about him in circulation there.[21] His political troubles were exacerbated all the more by his low productivity. Writers were by this point expected not only to refrain from negative comments but to contribute actively to the Five-Year Plan with inspiring portrayals of life and work in factories, at construction projects, and on collective farms. Babel dutifully wrote a few rather weak stories that convinced no one of his enthusiasm. Most of the truly valuable works of these last ten years deal not with the heroism of the new order but with Babel's own childhood and youth or with the early years of the revolution. His reticence became legendary. It was rumored that he was actually writing a great deal – one cartoon from these years shows him with a huge trunk full of unpublished manuscripts. The natural conclusion, of course, was that they were unpublishable, that is, counterrevolutionary. Babel was aware of this sentiment, and felt obliged to defend himself at the First Congress of Soviet Writers in 1934 as a "great master of the genre of silence," inspired, he says tongue-in-cheek, by a hypertrophied sense of respect for his readers.[22]

Babel was arrested at his dacha in Peredelkino outside Moscow on 15 May 1939. Numerous manuscripts were confiscated, among them several new stories and what may have been an almost completed novel. Only their now unlikely recovery can tell us for sure. Nor can we state with certainty exactly why he was arrested. The official charge, made more than a month later, was for "conspiracy of terrorism," one of the blanket accusations used in the purges. Speculations have included charges of spying, of Trotskyism, of making an insulting remark about Stalin. He was friends with the wife of Yezhov, the head of the secret police who was himself purged in 1938, and this may have played a role.[23] One might also conjecture that a writer whose fame rested largely on a work chronicling the humiliating defeat of the Soviet Army in Poland would not be particularly welcome now on the eve of the Soviet-German pact which gave Stalin the right to annex precisely the territories the Soviets had relinquished in 1921. Budyonny's First Cavalry, incidentally, was very much Stalin's personal creation.[24] In the final analysis, however, the exact reason is not really very important, for terrors operate on principles that defy both justice and logic.

For a long time Babel's date of death was uncertain. We now know that he was shot on 27 January 1940.[25]

Red Cavalry and the Polish-Soviet War

Relations between revolutionary Russia and the newly created Republic of Poland had been smoldering for more than a year before Babel arrived on the scene. They erupted into a major conflict in late April and early May 1920, when the Poles occupied Kiev, then the capital of the shaky Ukrainian People's Republic recognized by the 1918 Treaty of Brest-Litovsk. The principals are still debating whether the move was a preemptive strike prompted by fear of Russian designs now that the civil war had turned in favor of the Bolsheviks or an aggressive gambit to regain historically Polish territories. At any rate, the Soviets quickly responded to this challenge along a front extending from the Ukraine to the Baltic, and they were initially quite successful. By the end of May the Poles had been driven out of Kiev. By June they were steadily retreating, pursued in the south by Budyonny, in the center by Tukhachevsky, and in the north by Ghai. The offensive pressed on into July, and by mid-August the Red forces were threatening Warsaw in the center and Lvov in the south. They never reached either. The armies advancing on the Polish capital were repulsed by 20 August. Budyonny's cavalry suffered a decisive defeat on 31 August and was fortunate even to escape the so-called Zamoshch Ring. The Battle of the Niemen gave the Poles another decisive victory on the central and northern fronts in September, and by the mid-October cease-fire the Bolsheviks had been pushed back almost to their positions of six months before. The Treaty of Riga, signed in March 1921, was a victory for Poland, which gained a huge section of present-day western Ukraine and Belarus and considerable other indemnities. For Soviet Russia it was a painful defeat that would not be forgotten when borders were redrawn once again at the end of World War II.

No war is ever as neat and orderly as the generals' chessboards or the crisply sweeping arrows of a military map, but this particular conflict was messier than most. Norman Davies, who has written one of the most authoritative accounts, describes it as follows:

> Warfare in the Borders had a quality all of its own. The immensity of the theatre of operations, the impossibility of garrisoning it efficiently, turned the attention of armies to specific, limited objectives – rivers, railways, and small towns. Rivers formed the only lines of natural defence. . . . Fighting, for psychological as well as for logistical reasons, proceeded by fits and starts, jerking from one township to the next perhaps fifty miles on, like sparks building up energy in a terminal before jumping the gap. Action followed the lines of communication in a game of generals' leapfrog, back and forward between one station and another. . . . The line was too thin to be held for long. The flank was always exposed. To attack was easy; to retreat was always possible. . . . When the historian writes of "a general offensive" or "an advance on a wide front," he is rationalizing a thousand individual engagements. Border warfare was essentially local and fragmentary, spasmodic and infinitely confused.[26]

As guerilla wars in our own day may suggest, such mobile, fluid conflicts generate conditions that are more than usually conducive to excesses. Davies again:

> The fighting in the Polish-Soviet War was undoubtedly vicious. The Poles frequently shot captured commissars outright. The Soviets shot captured officers and cut the throats of priests and landlords. On occasion, both sides murdered Jews. The atmosphere was somehow ripe for atrocity. The soldier was surrounded by confusion and insecurity. He rarely found himself in a comfortable trench, or in the reassuring company of his regiment.

More often he was on his own out in the forest, or standing guard on the edge of a village, never knowing whether the surprise attack would come from in front or behind, never knowing whether the frontline had moved forward or back. Ambushes and raids bred panic, and invited vengeance. Meetings with the enemy were infrequent but bloodthirsty.[27]

Even allowing for exaggeration and unverifiable rumor, it is not difficult to believe that, for example, the entire Polish garrison at Zhitomir was put to the sword or that the hospital there containing six hundred Polish wounded and their Red Cross nurses was burned to the ground[28] or that in Grodno the Poles murdered sixty Jewish families, blinded seventeen young men, cut the breasts off women and raped young girls.[29] The stories of *Red Cavalry* abound in such violence against the defenseless. Particularly memorable and evidently common brutalities are the cold-blooded murder or mutilation of civilians ("Crossing into Poland," "Gedali," "The Life and Adventures of Matthew Pavlichenko," "Prishchepa's Vengeance," "Salt," "Afonka Bida," "Berestechko") and the killing of prisoners ("A Letter," "Konkin's Prisoner," "Squadron Commander Trunov"). Babel's campaign diary, which was never intended for publication, clearly shows that these incidents are not mere hearsay events inserted or embellished for the sake of fictional shock value. In one entry he relates the story of a pharmacist who was tortured by the Poles with a red-hot iron and needles under his fingernails.[30] The shooting of prisoners in another diary entry may well have served as the basis of the scene in "Squadron Commander Trunov":

There is a thundering hurrah, the Poles have been crushed, we ride on to the battlefield, a little Pole with polished nails rubs his rosy head and thinning hair, answers evasively, beats around the bush, bleats, well yes, Sheko [a commander] animated and pale: answer, who are you – I, he mumbles – a warrant officer, sort of; we are leaving, they take him away, behind his back a fellow with a handsome face loads, I shout Yakov Vasilevich! He pretends he doesn't hear, rides farther, a shot, the little Pole in underwear falls on his face writhing. Life is repulsive; murderers, unbearable, baseness and crime.

They drive the prisoners, undress them, a strange sight – they undress terribly quickly, shaking their heads, all this in the sun, a minor awkwardness, officers right there, awkwardness, just a tri- fle, though, through their fingers. I will never forget this treach- erously murdered "sort of" warrant officer.

Ahead – terrible things. We crossed the railroad at Zadvurdze. The Poles are breaking through along the rail line to Lvov. Attack in the evening near a farm. Carnage. We ride with a commander along the line, plead not to kill prisoners; Apanasenko [com- mander of the Sixth Division who replaced Timoshenko – Ed.] washes his hands. Sheko says casually, cut them down, this played a terrible role. I did not look at the faces; bayoneting, shooting, corpses covered by bodies, one is being undressed, another is being shot, groans, cries, wheezing, it was our squadron which mounted the attack, Apanasenko on the sidelines, the squadron properly dressed now, Matusevich's horse killed, he runs around with an awful, filthy face looking for a horse. A hell. The freedom we bring, terrible. They search the farm, drag people out, Apanasenko: don't waste cartridges, cut their throats. Apanasenko always says: cut the nurse's throat, cut the Poles' throats.[31]

It is artistically reworked scenes such as this which force even many of Babel's critics to concede that he succeeded in capturing the very special atmosphere and rich human interest of this war. To that extent the stories are true not in the external "but in the internal sense,"[32] surely the one that matters most to us. This is not to say that "external" truth should simply be dismissed as entirely irrele- vant, however, and here it is appropriate to address some questions that have been raised regarding the historical reality depicted in Babel's cycle. How much did he actually see firsthand, and how accurate are the accounts of what he claims to have witnessed? He was attacked on both points by Budyonny, who called him a "crea- ture of the army's back yard" who lacked substantial eyewitness experience of the action and was therefore ill-suited to judge the heroism of the Cossacks. Davies basically concurs, noting that with few exceptions, all the locations Babel mentions are twenty to thirty miles behind the front line at any given time, and that contrary to the impression given in the stories, "Babel much preferred to drink coffee with his Jewish friends in the taverns of Zhitomir and Berestechko than to ride into battle with his Cossack heroes."[33]

Certain comments are in order here. First of all, if Babel himself seldom actually came under enemy fire (he mentions his first battle on 17 August),[34] the extensive excerpts from his diary now available indicate that on numerous occasions he was much closer to hostilities than twenty or thirty miles. Especially as the Poles began to press the Soviets in mid-July, the headquarters to which he was attached switched back and forth just ahead or behind the enemy within the triangle around Brody, and he also seems to have been very close to the fighting in the advance on Busk.[35] As noted above, the front was in any case very mobile, and the rear, although undoubtedly much more secure, was probably not the cozy, tranquil haven detractors seem to imply. More important than the total number of engagements Babel may have taken part in or witnessed, however, is the philosophical question of what, exactly, should be defined as the essential "reality" of this or any other conflict. For understandable reasons, military commanders and historians perceive the locus of meaning in the actual fighting and the behavior of its participants, and in the impact of the outcome on further political and military decisions. That may be a legitimate and important view, but it is not the only possible one, nor is it the most productive approach to a work of imaginative literature. Babel was neither a soldier nor a historian; there is little reason, therefore, to be either surprised or disappointed that, like many artists before and after him, he has chosen to leave the military facts to others and to focus instead on the aspects of war that are most important to him: the effect of violence on human life, morals, and culture. As Viktor Shklovsky noted in Babel's defense during the debate, Budyonny was unhappy with Babel, but Kutuzov (the general who drove Napoleon out of Russia in 1812) would also have been unhappy with Tolstoy in *War and Peace*.[36]

That being said, it must still be admitted that in a few places Babel is not adverse to manipulating facts if he has compelling aesthetic reasons for doing so. Perhaps the most glaring example is in the very first paragraph of *Red Cavalry*:

> Comdiv six reported that Novograd-Volynsk was taken today at dawn. Headquarters moved out of Krapivno, and our supply wagons stretched out in a boisterous rearguard along the highway, the immortal highway running from Brest to Warsaw that was built on peasant bones by Nicholas I. (41)[37]

As Davies points out, the geography and chronology here are entirely inaccurate.[38] Budyonny's cavalry did indeed take Novograd-Volynsk, but the city is some two hundred miles to the southeast of Brest, which means that the "rearguard" would hardly be strung out in front to the west. Moreover, it was not Budyonny's but Tukhachevsky's forces that marched along this famous highway, and not in June (Novograd was occupied on 27 June) but in the first week of August as the Russians advanced on Warsaw.

There is more. Novograd-Volynsk is on the west bank of the Sluch rather than the Zbruch. It lies some eighty miles to the north of the latter river, which is nowhere near a line of march to the city. Budyonny's cavalry, in fact, probably never crossed the Zbruch at all, because the Dniester region to which it belongs was the responsibility of the Soviet Fourteenth Army under Uborevich throughout the summer of 1920. The error is repeated in the story "Italian Sunshine," where the narrator speaks of the "noiseless Zbruch" in the ravine below Novograd-Volynsk (64).

Wrong time, wrong river, wrong highway, wrong cities, wrong armies – one can sympathize with the historian who laments such "burglary" of history, but perhaps one can stop short of accusing the author of "gratuitous vandalism."[39] Babel's manipulation of his historical material is anything but gratuitous; nor are these alterations merely designed to convey "an atmosphere of apparent reality."[40]

After all, if that were the intent, surely he could have found some "real" facts that would have served just as well. The reasons for the discrepancies in this and a few other passages lie deeper, and must be considered in their full context to be properly appreciated.

Viewed from the broader perspective of European history, the Polish-Soviet War has been all but eclipsed by the larger conflicts that frame it, and perhaps for this reason it is easy to overlook its tremendous significance in the eyes of its participants. On the Russian side, the immediate contemporary issues at stake concerned the very survival of the revolution. Since at this point in time, at least, the Bolshevik leaders believed that Russia was not likely to endure unless similar revolutions were ignited in Europe, and since Poland lay directly in the path of any such spreading conflagration, the nature of the regimes in these border areas was of the utmost significance.

Poland was also an infant state struggling to survive, but was otherwise a very different country indeed. A parliamentary democracy ruled by men committed to Catholicism, private property, class interests, and patriotism, it was in many respects the exact opposite of Russia at the time, and the Borders were no less significant to Polish aspirations. This was the first time since 1772 that Poland had existed as a sovereign nation, and that was a gain its leaders were extremely anxious to consolidate, by territorial aggrandizement if necessary. Russia had more than once crushed such ambitions – twice in the nineteenth century alone – but even more distant history played an important role. Psychologically, the border areas were surrounded by a romantic aura of centuries past, when Poland stretched from the Baltic to the Black Sea and was the outpost of Christendom standing against the Turks and Tartars in defense of the Faith and warring with the Muscovites for control of the steppes.[41] The Russians made similar claims. Kiev was the cradle of Eastern Slavic civilization, and it had been ruled by Poland until late in the seventeenth century. In 1605 Polish forces took advantage of dynastic confusion in Muscovy to occupy Moscow and set their own candidate on the throne. This abortive attempt was followed by another in 1608, and not until ten years later were the foreign invaders finally completely driven out of Russia, marking the beginning of Russian nationhood. Added to this, of course, was the religious factor, for the Pope was regarded by many Orthodox as none other than the Antichrist.

To the principals, then, the conflict of 1919–20 was more than a border squabble. Babel skillfully exploits this emotionally charged, semimythical background in his opening paragraph to comment on the central issues raised in the cycle as a whole. The road from Brest to Warsaw, for example, was a symbolical high road to the heart of Europe, the road along which internationalist ambitions would most likely proceed. Russian soldiers had taken the route before – in pursuit of Napoleon, for example; in fact the very title of the story, "The Crossing of the Zbruch,"[42] recalls two poems by K. N. Batiushkov, who was with the army in that earlier campaign: "The Crossing of the Nieman by Russian Forces on 1 January 1813" and "The Crossing of the Rhine."[43] A Polish reader might instead recall the highway as a military road by which Nicholas I and his successors kept Poland in check after the abortive insurrection of 1830. The note that it was "built on the bones of serfs" further reinforces the political dimension – once a symbol of absolutist tyranny, the road is now serving to bring liberation from the social injustices of the past. (Or is it? The ambivalence of Babel's position will be discussed below.)

The River Zbruch serves a similar function. Although, as mentioned above, it played no role whatsoever in the taking of Novograd-Volynsk and seems to have been of minor importance throughout the war, it had considerable symbolical value as a border. First, it had been the boundary between Russia and Austria since 1772, and contemporary commentators made much of that fact as the Soviets pushed the Poles westward. I. Vardin (Babel's colleague on *The Red Cavalryman* and later among the most militant of his proletarian critics) wrote a leading article in August 1920 in which he declared to his readers that the old borders drawn by tsars and oppressors were no longer valid.[44] Second, there is the fact that the Zbruch was also reestablished as the border between Russia and

Poland by the 1921 Treaty of Riga. This immediately evokes what is
to become a dominant theme in the story and the cycle as a whole,
namely, doom and defeat, as the optimistic note sounded at the
beginning yields to more ominous allusions and imagery. In the
second paragraph, personifications of nature recall the Igor Tale,[45]
which is also a story of defeat, and the narrative goes on to present a
vivid picture of defiled nature, surrealistic details of blood, death,
and confusion, desecrated human dignity, cold-blooded murder. The
setting must also have raised questions in the mind of the contemporary reader as to the meaning of the entire conflict, since in context it
seems to be suggesting that at least as far as Russia is concerned, all
the suffering and bloodshed has really changed very little.

There are a few other "quasi-facts" – fictional details that are
deliberately made to coincide partially with real ones. Thus there
really was a squadron commander by the name of Trunov connected
with the story of that name; in fact Babel wrote his obituary for *The
Red Cavalryman*.[46] His first name, however, was not Pasha, as in the
story, but Konstantin; he was not killed in a duel with an airplane
piloted by an American (he calls him Major Reginald Fauntleroy –
his real name was Colonel Cedric Fauntleroy), and he is not buried
in Sokal. These details, of course, would not have been familiar to
the contemporary reader, who might, however, have heard of the
hero Trunov. Babel has taken an incident he probably knew only by
hearsay[47] and transformed it into an epic battle between one (far
from entirely positive) hero and a monster machine; or, if you will,
between the outdated swashbuckling of the past and the new cavalry
technology of the West.

In all these cases, facts have been tampered with in various de-
grees to serve thematic demands. Babel needed the symbolism of the
Zbruch and a duel with an airplane more than he needed accuracy in
details which for almost half a century no one seems to have noticed
anyway. The discrepancies, in any case, are not very numerous, and
the deeper truth that they help to convey is so consummately and
convincingly presented that even if other errors should come to
light, they are not likely to challenge the claim of *Red Cavalry* to

stand not only as the chronicle of this conflict but as the national epic of the Russian Revolution.

Red Cavalry: Notes on Style and Structure

Anyone at all familiar with *Red Cavalry* will probably agree that it is not the sort of work that easily yields its meanings on a first reading. There is a continual feeling that even that which can be readily grasped is somehow intimating or pointing toward something else that is possibly more significant, whereas at other places the text seems puzzling, ambiguous, or downright opaque. It is perhaps no wonder that so many different explications and interpretations continue to be offered. There is a very good reason for this difficulty: it is intentional and very much a part of the author's aesthetic and philosophical attitude. Babel is a modernist, an important exponent of the consciousness that dominated Russian art and literature between the last decade of the nineteenth century and roughly 1930. Central to the modernist aesthetic position is a shift away from the objective reality which the nineteenth-century realists had attempted to capture as unobtrusively as possible to a focus on the subjective vision of the artist and to the artist's material itself, which in the case of literature is of course language. This overall tendency was reinforced in Russia by the supremacy of poetry over prose during this period. The formerly rigid distinctions between the two became blurred as prose writers turned their attention to verbal fabric, exploring and exploiting its phonetic, semantic, and syntactical potential through rhetorical and prosodic devices, word play, the use of dialectal, archaic, and other distinctive lexicon, and the incorporation into fiction of all sorts of literary and nonliterary genres and discourses. Two of the innovators here were Aleksei Remizov and Andrei Belyi, who are often regarded as the seminal influences on the so-called ornamental prose practiced, besides Babel, by 1920s writers such as Evgenii Zamiatin, Boris Pilniak, and Vsevolod Ivanov.[48] Although there are considerable differences between them, all the ornamentalists display a penchant for phonetic, lexical, syntactical and structural devices that tend to undermine mimetic purpose and draw attention instead to the fact that before the reader is a consciously, deliberately, and painstakingly *made* work of art.

Compared to the prose of traditional realism, this prose is denser, more charged, more "poetic," more dedicated to evoking moods and associations than to producing recognizable descriptions of reality. Unfortunately, some of the most important devices contributing to this effect are phonetic and syntactical and next to impossible to demonstrate on the basis of even a very good translation, which, alas, the most commonly cited one by Walter Morison is not. Readers who have access to the original, however, can turn to almost any descriptive passage and discover some of these features for themselves. The second paragraph of "Crossing into Poland," for example, contains several interesting examples of alliteration, assonance, onomatopoeia, and sound orchestration. A syntactic and prosodic analysis would reveal a meticulously crafted arrangement of long and short clauses and sentences supported on a symmetric triadic structure and substructures. Reading and rereading such passages, it is easy to believe Babel's own report that an important stage of composition consisted in declaiming passages aloud to achieve optimal rhythmic and sonic effect.[49]

Other features can be captured more easily in translation. These include the use of repetition and parallelism, rhetorical devices, and imagery. Note, for example, the following sentences in the above-mentioned passage from the first story, which opens with three parallel subject-verb constructions using different subjects, then a triad of another three subjects in which one (Volhynia) is repeated and concluded with a pronominal reference:

> Fields of purple poppies bloom around us, the midday wind plays in the yellowing rye, virgin buckwheat rises on the horizon like the wall of a distant monastery. Quiet Volhynia curves, Volhynia moves away from us into the pearly mist of groves of birch, she creeps into flowery hillocks and with weakened arms entangles herself in thickets of hops. (41)[50]

Almost every story contains verbatim or slightly varied repetitions that heighten cadence and lyricism: "the ocean, the boundless ocean" (77); "rest – Sabbath rest" (78); "silence, sovereign silence" (119); "the tireless wind, the clean wind of night" (163); "the Sabbath, the young Sabbath" (193). In some places this sort of repetition extends to longer passages of equal or nearly equal material, as in the song refrain in "The Song" (188, 189) or the beginning and ending of "Squadron Commander Trunov" (143, 152).

Contributing to the pathos and emotional intensity of many stories are rhetorical apostrophes: "Destitute hordes roll on toward your ancient cities, oh Poland . . . woe unto you, *Res Publica*, woe unto you, Prince Radziwill, and unto you Prince Sapieha, who have risen for an hour!" (45); "O the rotted Talmuds of my childhood!" (69); "O Brody!" (82); "O regulations of the Russian Communist Party!" (127).

Babel is the acknowledged master of the striking image, which not infrequently relies for its effect on an original exploitation of color, sensory impressions, synaesthesia, animation and deanimation, and unusual combinations of the concrete and the abstract. Examples are far too numerous even to mention briefly, but one does not soon forget the orange sun rolling across the sky like a lopped-off head and the smell of blood and dead horses dripping into the cool of evening (42), blue roads flowing by like streams of milk spurting from many breasts (65), sponge-cakes spiced with cunning juice and the fragrant fury of the Vatican (43), bullets striking and swarming in the earth, quivering with impatience (87), the moon loitering like a beggar-woman in the sky (164).

Although a pull toward lyricism can be felt throughout the text of *Red Cavalry*, that is not the only defining feature of its language. Five stories ("A Letter," "The Life and Adventures of Matthew Pavlichenko," "Konkin's Prisoner," "Salt," and "Treason"), for example, are in what is known as *skaz* – stylized narrative imitating oral speech, often an incongruous mixture of styles resulting from the efforts of an uneducated speaker to use bookish language. Dialogue is infrequent, but many lines are in colloquial or substandard speech

whereas others are elevated. Still other passages are decidedly laconic, matter-of- fact, unemotional statements. In a manner typical of
Babel, these often convey very brutal material, which produces an
effect of striking incongruity. What gives Babel's prose its distinctive
quality is that these various registers and levels of discourse are so
often juxtaposed, several of them often occurring in the same story
or even paragraph. The result is a veritable mosaic of variegated
verbal fragments that forces the reader constantly to adjust his or her
inner ear to catch the fluctuating rhythms, accents, and flavors of the
language.

Reading such texts is of course more difficult than reading prose
in a more uniform key. What makes it even harder, however, is that
this contrastive mixture of language elements is not merely stylistic
pyrotechnics but reflects the overall principle on which the stories
are structured. This organization is in turn related to meanings and
says a great deal about the vision that underlies it. Carol Luplow
summarizes the main features of story structure in *Red Cavalry* as
follows: (1) a radically different proportioning of the three basic
story parts, especially an extended development of the exposition; (2)
a tendency toward nondramatic rendering of plot, where verbal elab-
oration dominates over even sometimes quite violent events; (3) a
weakening of causal and sequential links in favor of associational
connections between theme, imagery, and style; (4) a "kaleidoscopic"
arrangement of heterogeneous elements: inner tales, peripheral anecdotes, dreams, letters, notes, reminiscences, and so on.[51] All these
features represent departures from the "realistic," mimetic mode of
discourse, where narrative is more typically organized along spatiotemporal and causal progressions. In some respects, in fact, the
strategy represents a transition into the nonliterary medium of cinema: the stories of *Red Cavalry*, as one extensive monograph analyzes
in detail, are excellent examples of the cinematic technique of montage – the juxtaposition of disparate elements – which exercised an
enormous influence on modernist literature.[52]

We have already seen some of these techniques at work in "Crossing into Poland." The opening sentence begins in the voice of a

soldier recounting a recent military operation, perhaps in a newspaper report.[53] By the middle of the second sentence, however, an abrupt change occurs, with the introduction of a historical perspective ringing of revolutionary and nationalist propaganda as the Red Cavalry marches west to eradicate the social injustice of the Old World and Russia marches to reclaim her rightful territory from her ancient enemy Poland. This and the expectations aroused by the title seem to point toward victory.

The second paragraph marks an abrupt shift, as an intensely lyrical and subjective voice introduces a string of vivid images and sensory impressions that progress from dominantly visual at midday, to olfactory and tactile in the evening, to audial at night. The narrator is no longer only a soldier or a propagandist but an artist as well, and his incongruous voices already seem to suggest some underlying inconsistency in his character.

The third paragraph introduces another voice and viewpoint. The cavalry arrives in Novograd and the scene switches abruptly to the unnamed narrator and his quarters with a Jewish family. Noticeable here are two shifts – from the first-person plural "we" of the opening to the singular "I" in which the remainder of the story is told, and a palpable change of tone from lyrical description to a detached listing of the ravaged interior of the home. This is followed by the narrator's expression of disgust at the filth and his contemptuous description of the Jews hopping around "like monkeys, like Japanese in the circus."

These shifts in tone and voice are crucial to the theme we can now see developing. On the other side of the river, in both the literal and figurative senses, we begin to get a glimpse of war that has been stripped of the disturbing if colorful lyricism of the second paragraph. There is nothing at all "poetic" about overturned wardrobes, tatters of clothing, and Passover crockery desecrated (it seems to be suggested) by human excrement. The emerging narrator is also of interest. Until now he was a member of the military collective, its "voice," in a way, who seemed to be proposing to report to the world on its movements, set its exploits in the proper ideological perspective, and sing of its victories and defeats. Here he steps forth and begins to assume more individual contours. He still regards himself as part of the collective – his behavior toward the pregnant woman is insensitive at best, and he barely accords the other Jews human status. Yet at the same time is dropped the first clue that he is also a Jew. Who among his fellow soldiers would recognize the broken crockery used exclusively at Passover?[54]

The identity conflict taking shape in this passage is central to the overall theme of *Red Cavalry* and will be shown at work below in other stories as well. It is accentuated further here by another sharp transition back into a lyrical voice. In the oxymoronic image of the moon wandering about in the dead silence outside the window clutching her "carefree" head in her hands – a typical gesture of despair – we can sense the estrangement and loneliness hidden behind the narrator's mask of uncaring conqueror.

The next clearly demarcated fragment is a dream, itself a kind of inner tale or "text within the text"[55] in which the narrator sees the commander Savitsky – Comdiv six of the opening paragraph – shoot the eyes out of the brigade commander for retreating. Death draws closer still, as does the threat of defeat. The Jewess awakens him, for he has been tossing and turning and kicking the man "sleeping" in the corner. Following swiftly upon this is the horrible revelation, rendered even more striking by the laconic and matter-of-fact details with which it is conveyed, that the narrator has been lying the whole while next to the mutilated corpse of her father.

The final paragraph is yet another distinct fragment told in an entirely different voice, this time that of the Jewess. Her tale of the Poles cutting her father's throat is restrained, if not quite as dispassionate as the preceding section, but it and the story end in an emotional outburst that brings the tragedy and horror lurking below the surface to a concluding crescendo. The glaring contrast it provides with the rhetoric of the opening is itself a statement of a major theme, namely, the conflict between the forces of history and the fate of the individual.[56]

Beneath the seemingly fractured and disjointed surface, then, there are coherent themes and motifs, but it is largely up to the reader to find the relevant links. What of the work as a whole? Clearly, many stories can be read individually, and several of them have been anthologized as self-contained narratives. There is in fact some disagreement as to how the book is to be approached in its entirety, and depending on how vague or definite the connections between stories are perceived to be, observers have called it everything from a loose collection of stories, to a cycle of short stories, to a poem in prose divided into chapters, to an episodic novel, to a baroque novel.[57] The question of the exact genre of *Red Cavalry* need not be decided here, but there is more than intuitive evidence to recommend approaching it as a unity. From the beginning Babel conceived of his project as a single work of art, and not merely as a disjunctive series of stories that could be arranged more or less arbitrarily. He spoke with irritation of the material necessity that forced him to publish the stories separately: "To get money I've published in the local *Izvestiya* several wretched fragments, wretched precisely because they are fragments," he wrote a friend in 1923.[58] In his conversations and correspondence with his editor Dmitry Furmanov during the two years before the appearance of the first book edition, he repeatedly referred to the stories as "chapters" or "chapter-stories" (*glavy-novelly*), and he was personally responsible for their original order.[59] Furmanov reports that Babel described to him the final composition of the work as consisting of "at least twenty chapters which are already written and published, twenty written but not published – these will simply serve as links, cementing the others. Ten chapters are being written – these are long, serious chapters; they will present the positive side of the cavalry, fill the gaps . . . Altogether, fifty chapters."[60]

The components of narrative can cohere in a number of different ways. To return to a point made above, there is first of all the sequencing of spatiotemporal and causal events. As in the case of individual stories, this type of link is relatively weak on the level of the collection, but it is not insignificant. On the basis of direct or indirect references in the stories themselves and on a knowledge of the general movements of the First Cavalry, the stories as presented in the outline below follow a chronology broken by some flashbacks and flashforwards from mostly June (stories 1–9) through July and late August (10–28) to the end of August and into the middle of September (29–34). Story 35, added later, spans almost the whole campaign. These more or less correspond to the three stages of the First Cavalry's involvement – advance in June, advance with increasing resistance and some defeats in July–August, retreat in late August and in September – and they also tend to group in three general arenas: Novograd- Volynsk/Zhitomir, Brody/Berestechko, Zamoste/Chesniki (see map). As will be suggested below, these spatiotemporal blocks coincide with thematic divisions.

The datelines that Babel originally provided some of the stories tended to focus more attention on time and place of action or writing, but even then the unity thus created is fairly loose. Much more important than any such sequential principle is the associative one mentioned above, which relies on repetition or parallelism based on similarity or contrast. Among these devices may be mentioned recurring characters, recurring imagery, and repeated and varied themes, situations, subplots, and so on. Thus a majority of all the important and minor characters figure or are mentioned in more than one episode. To list them alphabetically: *Afonka Bida* ("Afonka Bida," "The Death of Dolgushov," "The Road to Brody," "In St. Valentine's Church"); *Akifiniev* ("Two Ivans," "Chesniki," "After the Battle"); *Balmashev* ("Salt," "Treason"); *Gedali* ("Gedali," "The Rabbi," "The Rabbi's Son"); *Grishchuk* ("Discourse on the Tachanka," "The Death of Dolgushov"); *Ilya Bratslavsky* ("The Rabbi," "The Rabbi's Son"); *Khlebnikov* ("The Story of a Horse," "The Story of a Horse, Continued"); *Kurdyukov* ("The Letter," "In St. Valentine's Church"); *Pan Romuald* ("The Church at Novograd," "Pan Apolek"); *Pan Apolek* ("Pan Apolek," "In St. Valentine's Church"); *Pani Eliza* ("The Church at Novograd," "Italian Sunshine"); *Pan Robacki* ("The Church at Novograd," "Pan Apolek"); *Pavlichenko* ("The Brigade Commander," "The Life and Adventures of Matthew Pavlichenko,"

"Berestechko," "Chesniki"); *Sandy (Sasha) the Christ* ("Sandy the Christ," "After the Battle," "The Song"); *Sasha* (the nurse) ("In St. Valentine's Church," "The Widow," "Chesniki," "After the Battle"); *Savitsky* ("Crossing into Poland," "My First Goose," "The Story of a Horse," "The Story of a Horse, Continued"); *Vinogradov* ("Berestechko," "After the Battle"). The significance of these recurrences should perhaps not be overemphasized – only exceptionally (in "Gedali," "The Rabbi," and "The Rabbi's Son," in "The Story of a Horse" and "The Story of a Horse, Continued," and in "Afonka Bida" and "In St. Valentine's Church") is there any real narrative connection between them. They do, however, invite us to look for thematic links between the episodes in which they appear, and they serve a cohesive function themselves by providing a familiar cast of characters.

Recurring imagery works in a similar fashion. Nature imagery is particularly prominent in this regard, and, among these many metaphors, the sun and moon are important both for providing a sense of temporal progression and for indicating psychic and thematic shifts. Thus we cannot help but notice the similarities between the colorful banners ("Crossing into Poland"), orange strife ("The Rabbi") and overflowing goblets ("Zamoste") of sunset, or between the moribund, roseate void ("Gedali"), ghost ("My First Goose"), and haze ("The Rabbi") of evening, or between the moon loitering like a beggar-woman ("The Widow"), the vagrant wandering outside the window ("Crossing into Poland"), and the homeless moon of "Pan Apolek." Structurally, these and other details create motif chains that provide atmospheric unity and cross-reference episodes. They simultaneously serve an important thematic function, as there is an observable tendency to link natural phenomena with certain types of thematic oppositions, and it has even been argued that such cadenced reappearances are intended to evoke a longing for the lost human involvement in the rhythmical patterns of nature and to suggest an almost paganly animistic universe.[61]

Themes, motifs, situations, and events echo one another throughout the cycle. One example discussed by van Baak is the important motif of crossing a river. Dominant in the first story, it recurs explicitly (although not as prominently) in "Afonka Bida," and implicitly in "Berestechko" and "In St. Valentine's Church." In all places it is connected with the notion of a threshold and the changes in character or perception accompanying the crossing of such boundaries.[62] Other such situations include Lyutov's inability to kill in "The Death of Dolgushov" and "After the Battle," which in both cases causes a rupture between him and the Cossacks; acts of revenge and revolutionary justice link "A Letter," "The Life and Adventures of Matthew Pavlichenko," "Prishchepa's Revenge," "Konkin's Prisoner," "Salt," and "Two Ivans"; Lyutov mistreats the women with whom he is billeted in "Crossing into Poland," "My First Goose," and "The Song"; Cossacks and their lost horses unite "The Story of a Horse," "Afonka Bida," and "The Story of a Horse, Continued"; old Jews have their throats cut in "Crossing into Poland" and "Berestechko"; prisoners are executed in "Konkin's Prisoner," "Squadron Commander Trunov," and (probably) "Two Ivans."

The role that these and other elements play will become more obvious as we attempt below to determine a more precise internal structure. First, however, a few words about the most important unifying element by far, which is the single consciousness that narrates or presents all the stories. The world of *Red Cavalry* is the narrator's world, and it is his biographical, cultural, and spiritual identity and experiences that select, organize, and refract the thematic material. Who, then, is he? The first-time reader of the work can be excused for not having an exhaustive answer ready, for even the external details are scattered in bits and pieces over the entire book. His name, Kirill Vasilevich Lyutov, is not entirely revealed until nine-tenths of the way through, and then not in a single story (the surname first occurs in "Squadron Commander Trunov" (146) and the name and patronymic in "Chesniki").[63] As can be gathered from explicit information supplied at scattered points, he is a Jewish intellectual from the south of Russia and a recent graduate of the Law School of St. Petersburg University ("Gedali," "My First Goose," "Discourse on the Tachanka"), which means he is in his early to mid-twenties. He claims his wife deserted him ("Zamoste"). He has served in the army for more than two years, since he fought against the Germans no later than March 1918 (the date of the signing of the Brest-Litovsk Treaty ending World War I for Russia; "Argamak"), and has been on the Red side in the civil war since at least the spring of 1919. He has taken part in campaigns in the Kuban against Denikin and the "Greens" (anti-Bolshevik peasant partisans), he may have gone through the siege of Uralsk in May–July 1919,[64] and he has evidently been with Budyonny's First Cavalry in the Caucasus, the arena from which the unit was transferred to the Polish front ("The Song"). Until shortly before the taking of Novograd-Volynsk, however, he was not attached to a combat unit ("Argamak"). The English-speaking reader should also be aware that the name Kirill Vasilevich Lyutov is very definitely Russian rather than Jewish, that there is considerable irony in the meaning of the surname ("lyutyi" = ferocious, savage, cruel), and that Babel himself used the pseudonym for his dispatches from the front. Again like his real-life namesake, Lyutov is attached to the army newspaper *The Red Cavalryman*. His official functions in that capacity include observing and reporting on the war and explaining the revolution to the soldiers, and at various points he explicitly or implicitly assumes these professional roles of reporter and political interpreter. He is never very convincing in either, however, because if he possesses the journalist's curiosity and keenness of observation and the agitator's flair for the pithy phrase, these talents are harnessed to a purpose that is emphatically aesthetic rather than informative or persuasive in nature. For Lyutov is above all an artist. He openly declares as much in "Pan Apolek," but his heightened aesthetic sensibility is overwhelmingly obvious anyway in his lyricism, his appreciation of both natural and created beauty, the strongly metaphorical mode of his vision, the important role he allots to dreams and imagination, the sensitivity he displays to sense impressions and the sensual phenomena of life, and of course the self-consciously crafted style of the narrative itself.

Lyutov's biography is thus sketchy at best. It is adequate, however, for he is not so much an individualized psychological portrait as a type shaped by the roles his background, situation, and temperament have imposed on him. All three of the main aspects of his persona – Jew, intellectual, and artist – define him as an outsider. In the reality of the 1920 war, of course, this is an entirely believable position, as Babel himself could personally testify. The type also has important literary antecedents extending back at least to romanticism and its estranged hero confronted with the contradictory need to identify with some larger collective or purpose without sacrificing his exclusive cultural, moral, and aesthetic sensibility. In Russian literature of the 1920s the intellectual hero torn between old and new was a common figure, and Lyutov is one of the most memorable of this series.[65] Emotionally and culturally rooted in the world of Jewish tradition and Western humanist values, he at the same time recognizes that that world is dying, and he wants to belong to the new reality promised by the Revolution. The bearers of the future are the Cossacks, and whereas he admires their vitality and masculinity, he is repulsed by their brutality. In its most basic contours, then, *Red Cavalry* is a work of quest for identity, understanding, and meaning on the individual, historical, and metaphysical levels, and all the component parts explicitly or implicitly address the questions that arise in the course of the search: ends and means, old and new culture and values, freedom and necessity, the meaning of history.

These and related contrasting and conflicting questions constitute the thematic heart of the cycle, and Lyutov's struggle to deal with them is what gives it cohesion and momentum. Obviously he does not move along ticking them off one by one – they overlap and merge, fade and reappear, are repeated and varied – and questions and possible solutions alike soon become blurred and ambivalent. Yet it seems equally unreasonable to conclude that they simply spill forth with no discernible pattern of internal arrangement, and it is legitimate to inquire whether some such organization cannot be discovered. One archetypal narrative structure is of course triadic, and there is reasonable evidence to suggest that such a principle is at work in this cycle; that is, if the stories are grouped into threes and compared in such units, the pattern that can be discerned seems clearer than what emerges from other possible arrangements. Even within this framework, of course, other variations are conceivable,[66] but the scheme shown in the outline below, with a break at "The Cemetery at Kozin" to be explained in due course, yields some interesting regularities.

Story		Place	Time
I	1 a) Crossing into Poland	Novograd-Volynsk	27 June
	2 b) The Church at Novograd	Novograd-Volynsk	July
	3 c) A Letter	?	?
II	4 a) The Remount Officer	?	?
	5 b) Pan Apolek	Novograd-Volynsk	late June–early July
	6 c) Italian Sunshine	Novograd-Volynsk	late June–early July
III	7 a) Gedali	Zhitomir	mid-June
	8 b) My First Goose	?	late July
	9 c) The Rabbi	Zhitomir	mid-June
IV	10 a) The Road to Brody	Brody	2–3 August
	11 b) Discourse on the Tachanka	?	?
	12 c) The Death of Dolgushov	Brody	1st week of August
V	13 a) The Brigade Commander	Brody	3 August
	14 b) Sandy the Christ	?	?
	15 c) The Life and Adventures of Matthew Pavlichenko	?	?
	16 The Cemetery at Kozin	?	?
VI	17 a) Prishchepa's Revenge	Leshniuv	late July–early August
	18 b) The Story of a Horse	Dubno	12(July?)
	19 c) Konkin's Prisoner	?	?
VII	20 a) Berestechko	Berestechko	6 August
	21 b) Salt	?	?
	22 c) Evening	?	?
VIII	23 a) Afonka Bida	Leshniuv, Berestechko	late July–6 August
	24 b) In St. Valentine's Church	Berestechko	7 August
	25 c) Squadron Commander Trunov	Sokal	?
IX	26 a) Two Ivans	Verba	22 July
	27 b) Story of a Horse, Continued	?	?
	28 c) The Widow	Busk	3d week of August

Story			Place	Time
X	29 a)	Zamoste	Zamoste	30 August
	30 b)	Treason	Kozin	August
	31 c)	Chesniki	Chesniki	31 August
XI	32 a)	After the Battle	Chesniki	31 August
	33 b)	The Song	Budyiatichi	?
	34 c)	The Rabbi's Son	Kovel, Rovno	September
	35	Argamak	Novograd-Volynsk Rovno, Budiatichi	June–August

Earlier events are the subject in 3 (early 1920), 15 (1918), 18 (spring [May?] 1920), 19 (May–early June 1920), 21 (May 1920), and 30 (4 August).

Within the general framework of the spatiotemporal unity described above, these triads tend to cohere through sets of thematic contrasts. One has to do with Lyutov's relationship to the worlds of Jews and Cossacks and Poles which he encounters, and these contrasts are often framed in terms of cultural, ethical, and moral values; another consists in comparisons of various characters in contiguous stories; still a third encompasses contrasts between reality and illusion, different aspects of which are the question of reality and art and the disparity between the reality and the rhetoric of war and revolution (both official and as expressed by participants). Certain generic similarities reinforce the triadic pattern in some instances. There may of course be more than one type of contrast in any group of stories, and many stories also cohere with others far removed from them. Also, the focus below on these links does not at all imply that those themes are the only or chief center of all stories, only that they serve as a kind of cement in a more complex structure.

1. *"Crossing into Poland"; "The Church at Novograd"; "A Letter"*

The opening story "Crossing into Poland" contains in embryo many of the themes of the book. Symbolically it enacts a crossing of the threshold from the "normal" world into one fragmented and tormented by ambiguity and contradiction. Past and present collide ironically in the first paragraph; oppressors and victims make their first appearance as Poles and Jews. The Cossacks are still an undifferentiated mass, but they are very much present. Here too is the fundamental ambivalence of the narrator, who on the one hand identifies with the "we" of the Cossacks and adopts the mannerisms of the conqueror, but on the other is probably a Jew himself and is in any case clearly disoriented by his new world. His inner state is projected onto the surrounding nature, which takes on a surrealistic aspect that blends with his nightmare to blur the line between dream and reality. As the focus of his consciousness moves from "we" to "I" there is an attendant shift from the faceless forces of history to the fate of individuals in its path, and that he chooses to end the story on the anguished cry of a pregnant woman speaks more eloquently than any overt declaration of his distressed reaction.

"The Church at Novograd" elaborates on most of these themes. The contrast between illusion and reality is now a major topic in this Gothic atmosphere of deceit, hypocrisy, and mystery. From the Jewish milieu of the first story the focus now shifts to Catholic Poland. The clash between past and present is felt on two planes. Echoing the opening paragraph of the cycle, an apostrophe shot through with irony and ambiguity is directed to this ancient enemy of Russia about to be overrun by the barbarian hordes from the East.[67] The conflict is also Lyutov's personal dilemma. The art of the church has a seductive hold on him, and he, as an agent of the future, must exert himself to break free of the decadent power of this past culture. He came as a stranger to the Jews in the first story. He is a stranger here as well, a "violent outsider" (*prishelets*); yet his protracted search for his comrades seems to suggest that his bond with them is also very tenuous.

"A Letter" breaks sharply with the first two stories thematically, generically, and narratively, yet in typical montage fashion it serves to illuminate them both. If the hesitation between illusion and reality was an important ingredient earlier and was connected with the narrator's vacillating perception and lyrical temperament, now that element is stripped away as Lyutov moves into the backgrounding frame of the story and relays the contents of Kurdyukov's letter to his mother "without embellishing . . . verbatim . . . in accordance with the truth . . . without changing a single word" (47). Vasily Kurdyukov emerges in every respect as the diametrical opposite of the narrator, who abandons the attempt to identify with the Cossack reality that now appears in detail for the first time. Lyutov's highly literary prose is supplanted by *skaz*. Every bit as striking as the shift in style is the mentality it is used to convey. Kurdyukov's world is confined to his horse, what he can put in his belly, and the exercise of physical force. His father's murder of his brother and his second brother's murder of their father are related almost casually, as just another of the sights he has seen away from home.

As is appropriate to an introduction, then, here are the main players and thematics: Jews, Poles, Cossacks; the lure of past culture and art versus the pressure of the present; the violence of history and the fate of the individual; the split, hesitant intellectual versus the monolithic mentality of the man of action.

II. *"The Remount Officer"*; *"Pan Apolek"*; *"Italian Sunshine"*

The fourth story begins the pattern anew with two stories wholly reflecting Lyutov's point of view followed by a third in which a letter introduces another narrator. A great deal could be said about the complex thematics of all three of these stories – in particular "Pan Apolek," which is in many ways the richest of the entire cycle[68] – but the focus here will be limited to some of the most apparent linking elements. The most prominent of these, developing the contrast between illusion and reality in the first triad, has to do with art and the imagination. All the main characters are artists or performers. Dyakov in "The Remount Officer" is a former circus athlete. He plays the part with gusto now as he prances before the crowd in his opera cloak and red, silver-striped trousers and cruelly mocks the peasants with his "miracle" of raising a horse from near death. There is of course a touch of irony in the portrait of this "graying Romeo," but his traditional Cossack panache sets him off from the oafish Kurdyukov, and this difference also serves to mark the boundary between the triads.

Dyakov's "art" is like the circus itself – mostly glitter and virtuoso tricks. Pan Apolek is more complex, although not in all respects

Dyakov's opposite. He is a heretic and a rebel, fusing in his art the spiritual and the physical, the Christian and the pagan – realms Church dogma has tried to keep separate.[69] His lowering of the elevated and elevation of the lowly in his new pantheon of saints is a heresy that fits exactly Mikhail Bakhtin's definition of the subversive role of carnival,[70] and it is little wonder that a modernist mentality such as Lyutov's should feel strongly attracted to it. One clearly senses the proximity of the narrator and the authorial position at this point, but Babel would not be Babel if it were left at that. Pan Apolek's art is in fact not as unambiguously positive as it might seem if we simply take Lyutov's initial outpouring at face value. First of all, if Apolek represents carnival in the Bakhtinian sense, there is a touch of the Coney Island huckster in him as well, and it is here that his connection with Dyakov becomes apparent. His offer to paint Lyutov as St. Francis is more than vaguely reminiscent of the mid-way photographer whose customers insert their heads into a selection of cardboard cutout bodies for their portraits. This leads to some vexing questions on the nature of art and its relationship to reality. Where is the line between creative transformation and leger-demain? And perhaps, after all, the artist is not quite as powerful as the members of the elite would like to believe. Apolek is *almost* the founder of a new heresy that *would have* challenged the Church, but in fact he remains an eccentric loner and rather enfeebled rebel who has left his vagabond life and can now sit comfortably in Pani Eliza's kitchen, tippling and telling stories. There is moreover something threatening in the demeanor of Pan Robacki, the crazed bell-ringer, who "yawns like a cat" and remarks that Apolek "will not die in his bed" (64). Perhaps lone heretics are not so very fearsome.[71] More important, perhaps art alone is not enough to resolve the contradic-tions of existence. This is the impression one gets from the conclu-sion of the story, which finds Lyutov warming up within himself "unfulfillable dreams and discordant songs" as he loiters along with the homeless moon on his way back to the sordid reality of his violated Jews.[72]

The line between fact and fancy, reality and imagination, becomes

blurred indeed in the next story, "Italian Sunshine." Surrealistic
dream imagery and theatrical metaphors permeate the work. Life is a
dream, all the world's a play, one is led to reflect of Sidorov and the
crazed drama he has written with himself in the lead role. Sidorov
combines Dyakov's flair for the histrionic with Apolek's colorful
imagination and rebelliousness, but he adds some elements distinctly
his own. He is a thwarted, poetic lover with a beautiful spiritual
vision of future peace. At the same time, he obviously loves bloodshed and considers murder the easiest solution to a problem. If he
cannot be sent to Italy to assassinate the king, he muses, perhaps his
anarchist rage over the cooling revolution can be of use to the
Odessa Cheka? Lyutov is both repelled and attracted to this enigmatic figure – repelled by his cruelty but attracted to his flights of
imagination, which betray an artistic nature not unlike his own. Both
Sidorov and Lyutov have recourse to their creative fantasies to trans-
form (or manipulate?) an unacceptable reality.[73]

If the first triad of stories presented some of the fundamental
conflicts and questions, the second extends these to include art,
which the man of aesthetic sensibility must always consider as a
possible solution. The result of this examination as presented here
raises the possibility that art falls short of being such a panacea.
Admiration tinged with irony in the first story moves initially to
affirmation in the second but then retreats into ambiguity. In the
third piece, the "divine madness" of the artist turns out to be not so
very divine – the imagination can be a source of death as well as a
source of life.

III. *"Gedali"; "My First Goose"; "The Rabbi"*
In the first and third stories of the next triad the scene shifts back
a week or two to the Jewish ghetto in Zhitomir. The second, "My
First Goose," is set among the Cossacks at an unspecified place, not
earlier than 19 July (the date of the Second Congress of the Comintern mentioned in the text) (75). Regarded on the basis of such
criteria it seems out of place, but as was noted above, spatial and
chronological links are often subordinate to thematic and other con-

nections. If Lyutov's kinship-detachment dialectic is taken instead as the basic organizing device, the coherence becomes much more obvious, for all three stories present a confrontation between him and the conflicting worlds of Jew and Cossack that he inhabits and that fracture his own personality.

Lyutov has thus far only indirectly revealed that he is Jewish, much less that he has an attachment to Jewish culture. In "Gedali" and "The Rabbi" we begin to appreciate for the first time the depth and complexity of that bond. On the one hand the Jewish world offers peace and love, harmony and security, and Lyutov the homeless waif longs to be received back into the bosom of the eternal mother of which Gedali speaks in the latter story. On the other hand, it is a moribund world of diminishing relevance to the present reality, a closed and stifling world locked into a dying past.[74] Despite his spontaneous sympathy, therefore, for the third time already he is a stranger here, and he understandably reacts to this alienation by stepping forth as a spokesman of the other, revolutionary reality: "We will cut open those closed eyes. . . . [The International] is eaten with gunpowder and spiced with the best-quality blood" (70, 72). The brusqueness of his remarks to Gedali, coming as they do on the heels of his poignant reverie, make the defensiveness of his position fairly obvious, of course, and we already have other evidence that his relationship to the revolutionary world is more complex than he would sometimes have us believe.

"My First Goose" drives this latter point home. If Lyutov is prevented by one set of allegiances from belonging to the Jewish community, his entire background estranges him from the Cossack collective. We have seen him groping for a sense of identity with these men, but this is the first time we witness him actively attempting to win their recognition and respect. The results are mixed at best: he does manage to blunt the most savage humiliation and gain a certain measure of tolerance, but the price is high. His adventure with the goose, which parodies both a heroic deed and a sexual conquest,[75] makes a mockery of his manhood. The closing image of his heart dripping blood over the killing (or murder – the Russian permits both translations) of the goose borders on a mawkish whimper that eloquently underscores the distance he must travel to integration with his comrades.

"The Rabbi" takes up where "Gedali" left off, the abruptness of the break with the intervening narrative serving to emphasize the duality of the narrator's consciousness. The ghetto is now viewed less sympathetically than in the earlier story. Gone is the charm of Gedali's shop and the instinctive attraction Lyutov feels for his humane ideals – the rebbe presides over a court of fools in a home that is described as a morgue inhabited by dying old men. Lyutov discovers another alien in the gathering – Ilya, the rebbe's son, described as a recaptured prisoner. Ilya is the last son of the rebbe, and the dynasty will end when he finally does break free. Lyutov hastens to leave and return to the glitter and bustle of the revolution, but from now on we know it can never claim more than a part of him.

iv. *"The Road to Brody"*; *"Discourse on the Tachanka"*;
"The Death of Dolgushov"

"The Rabbi" ends with Lyutov departing from one world by symbolically returning to the train. This concludes the first block of three triads. The next story finds him on the road, signaling the introduction of a second block that will continue until the next road ten stories later. Many of the same themes appear again, but now from a somewhat different perspective. Until now, for example, Lyutov's actual participation in events has not been very prominent. He has heard about violence or witnessed its effects, but his own action has been limited to the killing of a goose. In the first three stories here that involvement grows successively. In the first, he is an eyewitness to the destruction of the beehives; perhaps he even takes part himself. At any rate, it causes him great pain, for the bees and honey are symbolic of many things identified with the past and doomed to annihilation: order, altruism, compassion, spirituality, and wisdom.[76] The voice of the future is now Afonka Bida, who in his simple language paraphrases the official view that the destruction will give birth to a better world (assuming, of course, that its beneficiaries survive to enjoy it). The closing image of the war-ravaged Brody from which Lyutov and the Cossacks are forced to flee calls that vision seriously into doubt.

If Lyutov is distressed by the action of his comrades, however, he is temporarily comforted by a new closeness with them. He describes Afonka Bida's singing with evident sympathy and refers to the Cossack three times as "Afonka Bida, my friend," "the platoon commander, my friend," and "Afonka, my squad leader." Things get even better in "Discourse on the Tachanka." Lyutov has a driver; he is the proud master of a tachanka, that simple yet fearsome weapon of the steppe. He "has ceased to be a pariah among the Cossacks" (83), and there is newfound authority in the voice with which he describes the vehicle and his jaunts about the countryside. Yet even this delight is soon overwhelmed by the sight of the ruined synagogues. Like the story before, this one ends in a lament to the long-suffering Jews of Galicia and Volhynia, not as aesthetically pleasing as their southern kin but full of a "somber majesty" that cannot but command respect.

"The Death of Dolgushov" concludes this rising line with a sudden plunge. First, the fortunes of war are visibly changing. There was a hint of disaster in "The Road to Brody" and now it is realized, as a large Cossack force runs into stiff Polish resistance and suffers heavy casualties. Lyutov's paean to the tachanka rings hollow now, as the "stupid" cart bumps uselessly back and forth between the Soviet and Polish lines. Lyutov's seeming integration suffers a major setback, too, for none of the units want anything to do with him and his driver. Worse, now he is truly put to the test and asked to destroy, not a goose or a beehive, but another human being. He fails miserably – he cannot kill even to save a comrade from a more horrible fate. The way of peace, then, is not the simple solution it may have seemed, and there is truth in Bida's remark that "you guys have about as much pity for us as a cat for a mouse" (90). As for Lyutov's relationship to the Cossacks, his loss of Afonka Bida is only partially compensated by Grishchuk's gesture of sympathy closing the story. Only with the unusual among them – and Grishchuk is unusually mild – will he ever again be able to claim any kinship.[77]

v. *"The Brigade Commander"; "Sandy the Christ"; "The Life and Adventures of Matthew Pavlichenko"; "The Cemetery at Kozin"*

vi. *"Prishchepa's Revenge"; "The Story of a Horse"; "Konkin's Prisoner"*

Standing near the middle of the collection and flanked by two triads of stories focusing on Cossacks is "The Cemetery at Kozin," which generic and thematic criteria suggest can be separated from the surrounding material and posited as a center line dividing the cycle into two nearly equal halves.[78] It contrasts sharply with the stories preceding and following it, which cohere into two symmetrical triads. The shortest piece in the book, it is also the most static and impersonal, with the narrator present only as a camera eye focusing on a series of tombstones. These tell a tale of sorts, but – what is accentuated all the more by the intensity of the action in the stories immediately framing the piece – it is a cyclical rather than a linear story consisting of the single somber event of violent death visited upon the Jews over and over again down through the ages. The cyclical view of history that clearly emerges in this poem in prose can serve as a prism through which especially the immediately surrounding stories can be viewed, but in fact it is very near the philosophical core of the entire book; the distinctive generic and structural features of this story tend to underline the centrality of the theme even more. At various points – in the very first story and in "Gedali," for example – there is a sense that everything that is happening has happened many times before and will continue to happen many times again: there is nothing new under the sun. This is not the last time this theme will sound, and henceforward it will color all the events.[79]

If "The Cemetery at Kozin" is devoted to the fate of the victims of history, the six stories surrounding it present a gallery of agents of change. Their unity is not as simple as this may sound, however, for the six men described both conform to and diverge from received literary and mythical stereotypes, and here again we can discover a definite pattern in their arrangement. Elements of romantic Cossack legends are discernible in the portraits in the first stories of the triads (Kolesnikov in "The Brigade Commander" and Prishchepa in "Prish-chepa's Revenge"). A rather ungainly and undistinguished youth before his promotion and the victory, Kolesnikov now shows some true Cossack panache (swagger?) and can claim a place alongside the older warriors – "the famed Kniga, the willful Pavlichenko, the captivating Savitsky" (93). Prishchepa – boor, syphilitic, and fraud though he is – dresses the part of the dashing horseman and displays the passion and the ferociousness one might expect to find among a warrior nation. He exits the tale with a gesture straight out of a storybook, picturesquely casting a lock of hair into his burning home.

The second characters of each triad (Sandy the Christ in the story of that name, and Khlebnikov in "The Story of a Horse") depart in some significant way from the stereotype and as a result are much closer to Lyutov. Indeed, from what we have been shown thus far, it is almost difficult to believe that Sandy is a Cossack at all. His meekness and musical talent make him the spiritual kin instead of such characters as Gedali and Pan Apolek,[80] and like them he wins Lyutov's instinctive sympathy. As for Khlebnikov, his attachment to his horse is very typical, but his nonviolent, mainly verbal protest is not; nor is the aesthetic sensibility in which Lyutov senses a kindred spirit: "We were shaken by identical passions. We both looked upon the world as upon a meadow in May; as upon a meadow walked by women and horses"[81] (114).

The third story of each set contrasts sharply with its predecessor: set against Sandy and Khlebnikov are the far more violent figures Pavlichenko (like Sandy a shepherd) and Konkin, and the narrative shifts once again into *skaz*. In a mock-saga style promised by the title of the story, Pavlichenko tells how he spent more than an hour kicking his former master to death in front of his victim's crazed wife. The political commissar and thrice-decorated hero Konkin amuses his comrades with a tale of how he murdered a prisoner early in the campaign. These accounts are among the most violent in the entire work, and their effect is only intensified by the almost playful humor with which they are told.

VII. *"Berestechko"; "Salt"; "Evening"*

"We were on the march" (118) begins the first story; the change in geographical location underscored by the place name of the title and a shift in thematic perspective mark the introduction of a third set of three triads. "Berestechko" echoes and elaborates the theme of "The Cemetery at Kozin" in a series of montages that once again scrutinize the supposed meaning of history. Corpses on the burial mounds outside the city recall the disaster that produced the mounds centuries before, when war and the plague annihilated almost the entire population of Berestechko.[82] As in the earlier story, Bogdan Khmelnitsky, scourge of the Jews, is there in spirit, and there is unmistakable symbolic irony in the old man who crawls out from behind a gravestone to sing to the Cossacks of their past glories. The soldiers are greeted by barred windows and the announcement of Commissar Vinogradov's lecture on the Second Congress of the Comintern, which declared Russia the leader of the world liberation movement. This is followed by the unforgettable scene of a Cossack, "carefully, so as not to splash himself," cutting the throat of an old Jew (119). Friends and relatives are "free" to cart him off if they wish. Berestechko has been turned into reeking catacombs by war after war, and Lyutov climbs a hill overlooking the town to escape the depressing atmosphere. As he wanders "past walls where nymphs with gouged-out eyes were leading a choral dance" (121) he finds a hundred-year-old letter from a woman to her husband – probably an officer – asking whether Napoleon is dead and informing him that their own little future soldier is seven weeks old. In counterpoint with this throbbing refrain of death and war is Vinogradov's triumphant voice telling the "bewildered townspeople and plundered Jews" that they are in power, everything is theirs.

Skepticism toward the glory of the revolutionary cause rises to a new pitch here, and from this point we can see it arching from the very first paragraph of the book through "Gedali," through all the tales of brutality and plunder, through the victims in the cemetery at Kozin and the bringers of the violence – the Kurdyukovs and the Sidorovs and the Pavlichenkos and the Prishchepas and the Konkins.

The ironical juxtaposition of rhetoric and reality continues through the remaining two stories of the triad as well, and in both of them a question that may or may not have occurred to the reader is brought into focus, namely, how much of the revolutionary zeal we have seen arises from conviction and commitment to the cause and how much is merely rhetorical trappings for more basic and less noble human passions? This is a question that comes to mind in "Salt." A woman smuggling salt deceives "Soldier of the Revolution" Balmashev by pretending that the bag holds an infant, and he gallantly protects her from rape. Enraged when he discovers the deception the next morning, he takes his rifle and "washes away that stain from the face of the workers' land and the republic" (126). If, as has been pointed out elsewhere in partial defense of Balmashev, Pavlichenko, Konkin, and others, their anger is an understandable human reaction, it is also true that the patriotism and ideology of war and revolution offer only too facile lofty rationalizations for revenge, envy, and sadism. Balmashev's efforts to cloak his personal wrath in broken ideological jargon suggest that perhaps not even the actors themselves are fully aware of the boundaries of their true motives.

The concluding story of the triad, "Evening," is a sustained attack on rhetoric. The opening apostrophe to the regulations of the Communist Party and the dashing newspaper *The Red Cavalryman* is a Gogolian piece of hyperbole that achieves a similarly subversive effect. And who is it who lays the party's "dynamite fuse" beneath the gallant troops of the revolution? "Three bachelor hearts full of the passions of Riazan Jesuses" (127), all of them – wall-eyed Galin, consumptive Slinkin, and Sychev with his gnawed-away intestines – suffering from ulcerating, corrosive physical disorders (Lyutov's legs are also covered in scabby sores). Galin, the central character,[83] is the most sustained portrait of an ideologue in the book, and it is a telling one. He pines for the favors of the washerwoman Irina, but the formulas he rattles off from speeches and agitational handbooks cannot compete with the more direct approach of the fleshy cook Vasily, and Galin is aware of his physical inferiority. He is equally resentful of intellectual superiors such as Lyutov. One almost feels sorry for this rather pathetic figure, but there is another, far from harmless side to him that inhibits such a reaction. At the time *Red Cavalry* appeared, the real Galins were doing more than merely snarling at the "drivelers" they felt were claiming glory that was rightfully theirs, and it would not be long before they would pick up their "iron brush" and rub the Vasilys and Irinas and anyone else who needed it into shape as well. There is something very ominous about that flickering eyelid of Galin's as he preaches all this to Lyutov.

VIII. *"Afonka Bida"; "In St. Valentine's Church"; "Squadron Commander Trunov"*

One of the most obvious details marking the shift that occurs in the next group of three stories is the relatively expansive temporal and spatial structures of the first and third, which serve to set the triad off from its neighbors. "Afonka Bida" begins with a flashback to July, recapitulating events from a full twenty-one stories before (the battles around Brody), and ends with the entry into Berestechko on 6 August. "In St. Valentine's Church" depicts a single incident that takes place on the following day, but "Squadron Commander Trunov" moves to Sokal and has a ring structure: Trunov's funeral – flashback to the killing of the prisoners and the duel with the airplane – return to the funeral.

Some obvious and not so obvious links join these three stories. Afonka Bida is at the center of the first two, which also follow one upon the other. (This is the second of only three such sets in the collection, the others being "Gedali" and "The Rabbi," and "Chesniki" and "After the Battle.") The relationship of the third story to the first two is not so simple and hinges on a by now familiar juxtaposition of similar or different characters and plot elements pointing to some common themes. Once again we are confronted with Cossacks illuminated from contrasting perspectives that simultaneously confirm and challenge aspects of received stereotypes and myths. Thus we first find Bida mocking the peasant infantry and their rather incongruous Jewish commander. There is nothing redeeming about this behavior – he is quite simply a commonplace bully. Much more romantically appealing in their way are his despairing grief over the killing of his noble steed and the legends that arise out of the vengeance he wreaks upon the perpetrators of the deed. In the second story he and his comrades are back in the role of bullies desecrating a church. All in all, Bida comes off as a rather deromanticized hero, and perhaps his performance on the church organ is symbolic of the descent: in "The Road to Brody" his song floated like smoke above the squadron as they rode toward the sunset; now he sings incoherently in a drunken, cacophonous bellow.

Bully and hero are also Trunov's contrasting hypostases, but the stakes are considerably higher in his case, and we are given a closer and more vivid account of the violence. Complete with a stirring speech, flowers, gunfire salutes, and a playing of "The International," the hero's funeral opening the story is followed by a graphic description of Trunov's very unheroic murder of two prisoners. One, an old man, he impales on his sword, while he blows the other's brains out at twenty paces with his carbine. Had the story ended there, it would have been a fairly straightforward instance of deromanticization, but the remainder of the plot and some symbolism complicate the interpretation. Trunov and Vosmiletov, a Cossack who up until now has mainly been interested in plundering corpses, perish in a duel with four American airplanes, thereby distracting attention from the cavalry and probably saving many lives, including Lyutov's. Perhaps this sacrifice confers a tragic dignity on him and we are being asked at least to hesitate in passing judgment? Perhaps, but then again perhaps not, and here again the ambiguity arises from the doubt Babel very subtly allows to seep into perceptions of his characters' motives. Does Trunov's cruelty result from his "passion for justice," as has been suggested elsewhere,[84] or is there another possible explanation? Is his duel with the airplanes inspired by love and devotion to his men and the Cossack code, commitment to the revolution, or something else? First, it is difficult to find any "justice" in the killing of the prisoners. The ostensible military reason is to force them to identify their officers, but that is more a matter of convenience than necessity, and in fact Trunov is directly defying Commissar of War Trotsky's orders.[85] After killing the first prisoner, he threatens to shoot Vosmiletov for the much less serious offense of stealing Polish uniforms. He accuses the thief of betraying the young Soviet republic, but we have already seen that the charge of "treason" is not necessarily dictated exclusively by patriotism. Vosmiletov has disobeyed Trunov and thus challenged his authority, after all, nor should we forget that the property in question is war booty over which the squadron commander can be expected to exercise some proprietary control. More important, however, is our evaluation of Trunov's encounter with the enemy. The battle is so hopelessly unequal that it seems almost a deliberate suicide. Here one cannot help recalling the enigmatic figure of the Galician Don Quixote walking through the town earlier in the story.[86] Perhaps Trunov is similarly a kind of crazed victim of his own heroic fantasies. Here as well is another link to Afonka Bida in the first story, whose frenzied forays are described as "despairing, lone wolf attacks" on a massive enemy (136). The line between heroism and pathology is becoming rather blurred.

Another important theme in these stories merits some comment, for it is implicitly present throughout the work. It has to do with the status of law in the extreme circumstances of war. On a broader level it concerns the whole notion of justice and how and by whom it is to be done. Lyutov, it will be remembered, is himself a graduate of law school and can be expected to be more than usually sensitive to such issues. In both "In St. Valentine's Church" and "Squadron Commander Trunov" he appears in a new and active role as the spokesman of civilized legality. He reports the desecration of the church to his superiors and announces that the offenders were brought before a court-martial. In the latter story he has an altercation with Trunov over the prisoners, insisting that the commander follow the orders pertaining to their treatment. Considering the characters of the men he confronts, these are truly courageous acts and must surely mitigate the charge of moral cowardice that has sometimes been leveled at him. How effective this courage is against such outrages is more ambiguous. Lyutov neglects to inform us of the sentence passed down by the court, and since he also notes that the church was closed, the verdict was in any case hardly a victory for the populace. The only result of his conflict with Trunov seems to have been to earn him the hostility of the other Cossacks. "Justice," it would seem, is defined and done by the strong, and laws, orders, and other civilized niceties can be enforced or ignored at will.

IX. *"Two Ivans"; "The Story of a Horse, Continued"; "The Widow"*

Justice and the law are also a shared theme in the next set of three stories. "Two Ivans" picks up where the preceding triad left off and leads to some of the same conclusions. One Ivan, the deacon Aggev, feigns deafness to escape service at the front and is to be sent to the rear for tests. He is turned over to Ivan Akinfiev, who, after having a bit of "sport" with him, very obviously is going to murder him before they reach their destination. Lyutov makes no protest here, but his attitude toward what he sees happening is amply evident anyway. To have any understanding at all for Akinfiev's deed, we must be convinced that it is necessary under the circumstances, that Aggev is a coward as charged, and/or that it is warranted by some larger purpose. None of this receives much support here. Akinfiev alone decides Aggev must die. The deacon is most certainly not a coward, for he faces his almost certain death with dignity. What he very well may be, however, is a pacifist whose only choice to refuse to kill is to feign disability. Lyutov (this will become even more evident later) holds similar views. He calls the corpse of the Pole on whom he inadvertently urinates "my unknown brother," whereas his comrade Akinfiev only "chances" to be his bedfellow (155–56). As for the noble end justifying these violent means, are we really to believe Akinfiev's defense of his contemplated act (those who know him do not!), or is he, as Barsutsky notes, simply an "animal"[87] (154) who, like so many before him, is taking advantage of the situation to indulge his own sadism? There are also the observations of Lyutov himself, who stops to focus on the fields sown with excrement and reports a comment that perhaps more eloquently than any other passage in the book summarizes his view of this reality: "We call ourselves human beings, yet we're worse than jackals with our filth. You're ashamed for the earth" (159).

"The Story of a Horse, Continued" seems at first to soften this unrelieved picture of savage justice. Khlebnikov appears reconciled to the loss of his stallion and writes Savitsky a letter to that effect. But is he really so mellow? Living now in Vitebsk, Khlebnikov is president of the district revolutionary committee, which at the time meant he was in charge of revolutionary "discipline" in his area. "Keeping an eye on the local authorities and on district units in terms of administration" (161), one reflects, is just the sort of job Sidorov or Galin would relish.

There is a legal issue at the center of "The Widow" as well. What begins as the last will and testament of the dying commander Shevelev degenerates into a squabble between one of his "heirs," his "wife" Sasha (the platoon concubine), and Levka, the "executor" of the estate, over the ownership of a stallion and some medals and underwear. The horse is to go to the regiment and the rest to Shevelev's mother. As it turns out, Sasha seems to have gotten the stallion (from the commander, her new "husband"?) and is evidently reluctant to part with anything else either. The matter is settled in typical Cossack fashion with Levka smashing his fist into the woman's face to force her to follow the dead man's wishes. Formally Levka is right, but the probity of his motives is not entirely above suspicion. A generally unsavory character, he fancies himself something of a ladies' man and had designs on Sasha himself, and as he relates his exploit and promises to repeat it, his "shining eyes" seem to betray a by now familiar blend of righteous indignation and sadistic pleasure.

x. *"Zamoste"; "Treason"; "Chesniki"*

Nowhere is *Red Cavalry* particularly bright or comforting, but there is a palpable darkening of atmosphere in the second half of the book. Violence and brutality are depicted more vividly and starkly than earlier, and the heroic ethos has been tarnished again and again by suggestions that it is inextricably bound up with narrow egotism, sadism, perhaps even mental instability. Rhetoric rings hollow; it too masks and is confused with the basest motives. "Zamoste" – once again there is a shift in location underscored by the geographical name – marks the beginning of the final phase of this progressive deterioration. The story is saturated with surrealistic imagery: drowned mice and cadaverous trees under a sky of chloroform; a feverish dream of naked breasts and a corpse. Disaster is near, defeat is imminent, the campaign is lost, and realization of this fact lies like a pall over all the remaining stories. Victors and vanquished both prepare to settle accounts. The Poles launch a pogrom of the Jews in Zamoste. The act is applauded by Lyutov's peasant comrade, since the traitorous Jews are to blame for everything (170), and genocide is the obvious answer. "Treason" is also the subject of the last *skaz* narrative in the cycle, Balmashev's letter echoing a theme from the first, where the "dirty Yids" tried to resist Cossack justice by following Trotsky's orders (50). Once again we hear the voice of a disgruntled militant who, when demobilized, will claim that the revolution has been betrayed. The names of the doctors Balmashev is accusing more than vaguely suggest that the Jews will be given special attention. Gedali was closer to the truth than even he imagined.

The triad ends with the Cossacks charging off to meet the Poles in the "unforgettable attack at Chesniki" (182). There can be little doubt as to the outcome, for in the shadow of the defeat just predicted and the sight of the bedraggled, hesitant Cossacks, Voroshilov's cry "On to Warsaw!" and his revolutionary and nationalist rhetoric seem not only hollow but downright pathetic. This constitutes roughly half the story. The other half is devoted to the episode in which Sasha has her mare covered by the Divisional Commander's thoroughbred stallion. The juxtaposition of this trivial and earthy incident with more significant historical events is open to several interpretations: it has the effect of lowering the stature of the latter, it is a typical Babelian mixture of violence and sex, and it may suggest that life will continue, even in the very midst of death and destruction.

XI. *"After the Battle"; "The Song"; "The Rabbi's Son"*

The final triad of stories is valedictory in both tone and substance. The postlude is announced in the very title of the first – the battle, indeed the war, is lost, and the closing story of the original thirty-four finds the First Cavalry retreating back into Russia. Lyutov, who has remained in the background during the preceding six stories, now reemerges for the last time to focus attention on his emotional and ethical dialectic. After the battle of Chesniki he reaches the nadir in his estrangement from the Cossacks. Akinfiev, that agent of revolutionary justice (it is surely no coincidence that he is identified twice as the driver for the Revolutionary Tribunal), denounces him as a traitor for riding into battle with an unloaded gun. It is uncertain how he has come by this information or whether it is in fact true, but Lyutov in any case does not deny the charge. The more important point is that Akinfiev has correctly intuited Lyutov's character, as he evidently correctly sensed Ivan Aggev's in the earlier story. Lyutov is – what has been suggested indirectly for some time now – a pacifist, perhaps even a religious believer, and this throws the Cossack into a murderous rage. Whether the source of that wrath is a sense of wounded justice or merely Akinfiev's sadism is once again a matter of interpretation. We may, however, reflect that such charges were soon codified in official discourse as "abstract humanism," a club that served to rid the regime of more than one bothersome intellectual. As for Lyutov, his concluding lament over his inability to kill is in a by now familiar self-pitying and ironic vein, but at its core is a thoroughly serious desire to fit into the world he inhabits. If he could, he would readily violate the moral sensibility that condemns him to remain on the lonely periphery.

He cannot, however, and "The Song" only serves to reveal even further how insurmountable is the task. He makes one final effort to play the part of the aggressor when he threatens the landlady with his revolver to obtain food, but since the revolver is probably not even loaded he is even less convincing than earlier. At bottom he is the spiritual brother of Sandy the Christ, and in a pattern we have seen before he now moves toward him. The stars, the fields, home, a mother's love – these are the emblems of eternity that command his true allegiance. For a brief poignant moment, the art and the love in Sasha's singing soften the brutality, ease the pain, evoke dreams of a world ruled by compassion rather than hate. Perhaps this tender interlude so near the end of the cycle seems to be saying that they will always remain only dreams, but they will remain.

"The Rabbi's Son," the story that originally concluded the cycle, is among the most enigmatic and ambiguous of all. If Lyutov has been seen moving away from the likes of Akinfiev and then back to Sandy the Christ, here he is once again searching for contact with his Jewish identity. The first lines hark back to the beginning of the campaign in Zhitomir described in "Gedali" and "The Rabbi." Two riddles present themselves almost immediately. First, who is this Vasily to whom Lyutov addresses the opening apostrophe? His name is definitely Russian. Is he using it like Lyutov to conceal a Jewish identity? If not, what is he doing accompanying Lyutov to Rebbe Motale's house on the Jewish Sabbath? Or did he accompany him? There is no mention of anyone else in the earlier story. On the contrary, Lyutov states that "Gedali led me" (78), and he leaves alone to return to the train after the supper.[88] There are more discrepancies connected with the entire scene and especially with the title character, Ilya Bratslavsky. Although details such as the horses neighing and Cossacks shouting outside the window coincide exactly in both stories, in "The Rabbi" Ilya is described as a "rebellious" (*nepokornyi*) son; his face is "consumptive," and he sits (blasphemously) chain-smoking during the prayer service in a stark setting almost devoid of furnishings. Mordecai contemptuously snatches a cigarette out of his mouth and spits in his face. As the scene is later recalled, in very sharp contrast, Ilya takes part in the ritual. His "expressionless (lifeless), humble (*pokornoe*), beautiful" face hovers in the candlelight above the Ark and the Torah, whose scrolls are wrapped in purple velvet (191).

Considering that this story is among those of the cycle that has received the most attention, the notice given to these puzzling differences has been rather slight and of very recent date. Thus explaining the discrepancies as being the result of "a not entirely precise" memory[89] makes them seem like minor errors of detail, when in truth they are contradictory. Perhaps the later account of the scene has been affected by the fact that Ilya is dead, and Lyutov's sense of bereavement finds expression in his description of him as he was when still within his father's world.[90] That seems psychologically plausible enough, although even then the embellishment seems a bit extravagant.

The identity of Vasily is even more vexing. Suggested solutions have been either that he is a non-Jew and so alien as to be unable to understand the story being told[91] or that he is "an alter ego [also a Jew hiding behind a pseudonym] whose similarity to Lyutov reconciles the apparent contradiction between saying that one or both were taken to the rebbe's."[92] Presumably this means either that a real Vasily was with Lyutov in some abstract sense, if not physically, or that Vasily is some sort of imagined half of Lyutov – a masked "Russian" half being addressed by the Jewish half, which is now being exposed. (Lyutov's assumed patronymic Vasilevich – son of Vasily – has just been revealed, which may or may not serve to reinforce this connection.)

What of Ilya, the "last prince" of the dynasty and the man Lyutov calls his "brother"? Here again various interpretations are possible. On the one hand it is claimed that he is Babel's construction of a perfect man combining Jewish intellect and Cossack valor, and that this fusion is represented symbolically by the contents of his trunk: Maimonides and Lenin; Hebrew poetry and revolutionary pamphlets; cartridges and phylacteries.[93] On the other hand it can be argued that this is no real fusion at all, but merely a hodge-podge of incompatibilities not unlike the cultural and emotional baggage carried by Lyutov himself, and that Ilya's death and burial at a "forgotten station" hardly seems to suggest he has left much of a legacy to the world.[94] Unless, as a third argument, the last breath that Lyutov receives is interpreted to mean that Ilya has passed on his inspiration (the connection between the Russian *vzdokh* – a sigh = inhalation (*vdokh*) and exhalation – and inspiration (*vdokhnovenie*) is much more

transparent than in the similar etymology of the English word).[95] In
that case the whole of *Red Cavalry*, with its tortured, often faltering,
perhaps impossible search to unite revolution and justice, violence
and love, Jew and Russian and Cossack and Pole, is part of the
heritage conveyed to us, the readers, who are left to ponder its
significance in our own lives and history.

This latter point is just one possible reading, of course – "The
Rabbi's Son" is so riddled with ambiguity that one hesitates to say
anything much more definite – but no interpretation yet suggested
gives much sense of closure to the cycle, and perhaps that is much of
the point. Thematic and philosophical irresolution, as Carol Luplow
notes, is central to the world of *Red Cavalry*,[96] and clear solutions
would be destructive of that purpose. "Argamak," added in 1931,
may stress this quality even more. Babel never explained why he
decided to include the story, and the usual assumption is that, possibly in response to political pressure,[97] it was inserted to provide a
somewhat less somber ending by showing Lyutov at last attaining a
measure of acceptance among the Cossacks.[98] First of all, it is difficult to agree with that conclusion. Lyutov does not win the friendship of the Cossacks – the most he achieves is a kind of welcome
anonymity when he learns to ride well enough to avoid their contemptuous stares.[99] On a more meaningful level he is as estranged as
ever from them. Baulin, one of those men we have already met who
never doubt the correctness of their path, snarls at Lyutov: "You're
trying to live without enemies. That's all you think about" (200).
Afonka Bida or Akinfiev could not have said it better. More important, the story is not really an ending at all – it spans the entire cycle
chronologically, beginning before any of the other stories with
Lyutov's transfer to the Sixth Division, and ending in the village of
Budiatichi, which is mentioned in "The Song," the penultimate narrative. It also reemphasizes the split in the narrator's character and
his desire to fit with the Cossacks, which seemed to yield in the final
triad to forces working in the opposite direction. Although it is easy
to locate it as preceding and paralleling almost the entire collection,
its highlighted position at the very end appears to be suggesting that

the issue has not been resolved, that there is no easy reconciliation between the powers which tug in different directions on Lyutov's imagination, his emotions, and his conscience. Babel offers no clear answers, either to the dilemmas that plague his narrator or to the similar crises of values that have helped define our twentieth century. But he has done what Anton Chekhov once declared to be the only genuine mission of the artist – he has asked some very relevant questions.

NOTES

1. The most complete collection of Babel's works is his *Sochineniia* in two volumes (Moscow, 1990), of some thousand pages, which includes all his stories and plays, a couple of film scripts, his 1920 diary, much of his journalism, a substantial collection of letters, and some of his infrequent public statements.

2. Nathalie Babel's account is in Isaac Babel, *The Lonely Years, 1925–1939*, translated by Andrew R. MacAndrew and Max Hayward, edited and with an introduction by Nathalie Babel (New York: Farrar, Straus, 1964); the most recent collection of memoirs is the reprinted and expanded 1972 edition of *Vospominaniia o Babele* (Moscow: Izd-vo "Knizhnaia palata," 1989), edited by Babel's second wife, A. N. Pirozhkova.

3. The most extensive biography is Judith Stora-Sandor, *Isaac Babel'. L' homme et l'œuvre* (Paris: Klincksieck, 1968). Accounts based on archival sources are L. Livshits, "Materialy k tvorcheskoi biografii I. Babelia," *Voprosy literatury* 4 (1964), 110–35, and U. Spektor, "Molodoi Babel'," *Voprosy literatury* 7 (1982), 278–81.

4. Spektor, "Molodoi Babel'," 279.

5. I. Babel, "Autobiography," in *The Lonely Years*, xii–xiii.

6. See Spektor, "Molodoi Babel'," who suggests that he may have remained in Saratov until 1916.

7. His experiences may be reflected in the four stories of "On the Field of Honor" (1920), which are based on Captain Gaston Vidal's *Figures et anecdotes de la Grande Guerre*. The English translation is in Isaac Babel, *You Must Know Everything*, translated by Max Hayward, edited and with notes by Nathalie Babel (New York: Farrar, Straus and Giroux, 1969). On the relationship between these stories and *Red Cavalry*, see C. D. Luck, *The Field of*

Honour: An Analysis of Babel's "Na pole chesti," Birmingham Slavonic Monographs No. 18 (University of Birmingham, 1987).

8. Babel', *Sochineniia*, vol. 2, 372–73. The most detailed treatment thus far of Babel's connections with the secret police is S. Povartsov, "Isaak Babel': portret na fone Lubianki," *Voprosy literatury* 3 (1994): 72–96.

9. Babel, *The Lonely Years*, xiv.

10. Babel', *Sochineniia*, vol. 2, 372. A dramatized (but completely unsubstantiated) account of Babel's work with the Cheka is in M. Skriabin, *Svetit' mozhno, tol'ko sgoraia* (Moscow: Politizdat, 1987), 307–10.

11. James Falen, *Isaac Babel: Russian Master of the Short Story* (Knoxville: University of Tennessee Press, 1974), 24.

12. Agnes Gereben, "Isaac Babel's Diary and His 'Red Cavalry,'" *Hungaro-Slavica, IX. Internationaler Slavistenkongress, Kiev, 6–13 September 1983* (Cologne-Vienna), 55–59.

13. See Carol Avins, "Kinship and Concealment in *Red Cavalry*," *Slavic Review* 53, no. 3 (Fall 1994): 696–97, for a discussion of this question. The conjecture that Babel mistakenly wrote a roman *vi* instead of *vii* for the month explains the first entry, but the first four entries?

14. Konstantin Fedin, *Gor'kii sredi nas* (Moscow: Molodaia gvardiia, 1967), 216.

15. S. Budennyi, "Babizm Babelia iz 'Krasnoi novi,'" *Oktiabr'* 3 (1924): 197. The title contains a derogatory pun on Babel's manliness ("babizm" = "womanishness"). On the confrontation with Budennyi, see G. S. Merkin, "S. Budennyi i I. Babel' (k istorii polemiki)," *Filologicheskie nauki* 4 (1990): 97–103.

16. I. E. Babel', *Stat'i i materialy* (Leningrad: Academia, 1928). Reproduction by Prideaux Press (Letchworth, 1973).

17. Budennyi's letter and Gor'kii's reply are in Babel, *The Lonely Years*, 384–89.

18. This is reported in the memoirs of a Yugoslav writer who stayed at Babel's house during a trip to the Soviet Union in 1936. Ervin Sinkó, *Roman eines Romans* (Cologne: Wissenschaft und Politik, 1964), 315.

19. Babel, *The Lonely Years*, 61, 84.

20. Babel was, however, genuinely interested in the cinema, and as will be pointed out below, his style owes much to cinematic techniques. For a list of the scripts he worked on, see Sicher, *Style and Structure in the Prose of Isaac Babel'*, 41–45.

21. Babel, *The Lonely Years*, 239. The situation was exacerbated by the publication of a probably spurious interview in the Polish weekly *Literary News* quoting Babel's critical remarks on the Soviet Union. He was forced to defend himself before the board of the Writer's Federation (see Babel', *Sochineniia*, vol. 2, 372–74), and it was here, incidentally, that he seems to have exaggerated his role with the Cheka.

22. Babel', *Sochineniia*, vol. 2, 381.

23. On Babel's confiscated and lost texts, see V. Kovskii, "Sud'ba tekstov v kontekste sud'by," *Voprosy literatury* 1 (1995): 47–62.

24. Norman Davies, *White Eagle, Red Star. The Polish-Soviet War, 1919–1920* (New York: St. Martins, 1972), 117.

25. A. Vaksberg, "Protsessy," *Literaturnaia gazeta*, 4 May 1988, 4.

26. Davies, *White Eagle, Red Star*, 35–36.

27. Ibid., 38. Jews were murdered more than "on occasion": between 1918 and 1921, pogroms in the Ukraine claimed 60,000 killed, 100,000 wounded, and 200,000 orphans (Nora Levin, *The Jews in the Soviet Union since 1917*, vol. 1 [New York: New York University Press, 1988], 43). Babel wrote about atrocities by both sides in articles for *The Red Cavalryman* ("The Unvanquished Killers" and "Knights of Civilization"). For an account of Babel's position and a translation of the articles, see Efraim Sicher, "The 'Jewish Cossack': Isaac Babel in the First Red Cavalry," *Studies in Contemporary Jewry: An Annual*, vol. 4 (The Jews and the European Crisis, 1914–1921), edited by Jonathan Frankel (New York: Oxford University Press, 1988), 113–34. The Russian text is in Babel', *Sochineniia*, vol. 1, 203–6.

28. Davies, *White Eagle, Red Star*, 125.

29. Joseph Roth, *Berliner Saisonbericht* (Cologne: Kiepenheuer and Witsch, 1984), 45.

30. Isaak Babel', *Socheniniia*, vol. 2, 403–4 (diary entry of 7 August).

31. Babel', *Sochineniia*, vol. 2, 415–16 (diary entry of 18 August). See also the original version of the Trunov episode "Ikh bylo deviat'" (Babel', *Sochineniia* vol. 1, 437–39), translated as "And Then There Were None" in Isaac Babel, *You Must Know Everything. Stories 1915–1937*, translated by Max Hayward, edited with notes by Nathalie Babel (New York, 1969), 125–34.

32. Norman Davies, "Izaak Babel's 'Konarmiya' Stories, and the Polish-Soviet War," *Modern Language Review* 67, no. 4 (1972): 848.

33. Davies, "'Konarmiya' Stories," 848–49.

34. Babel', *Sochineniia*, vol. 1, 415.

35. See Babel', *Sochineniia*, vol. 1, 378–401, 410, 418.

36. Quoted in G. S. Merkin, "S. Budennyi i I. Babel' (k istorii polemiki)," *Filologicheskie nauki* 4 (1990): 97–103.

37. My translation. Here and in numerous other places the most commonly used English edition leaves much to be desired. Numbers in parentheses within the body of the text are to the corresponding passages in *The Collected Stories of Isaac Babel*, translated by Walter Morison (New York: New American Library, 1974). The phrase "the immortal highway" (*po neuviadshemu shosse*) was later deleted by Babel.

38. Davies, "'Konarmiya' Stories," 848.

39. Ibid.

40. Ibid., 849

41. Davies, *White Eagle, Red Star*, 29.

42. In one of many examples of insensitivity to the patterns of the text, the title of the story is rendered by Morison as "Crossing into Poland," which completely conceals the original intent. Several other titles tamper with the original: "Rabbi" in "The Rabbi" and "The Rabbi's Son" should read "Rebbe," as this is a much different, charismatic type of Hasidic leader. (Most scholars have perpetuated the error in their studies.) "Prishchepa's Revenge" and "Konkin's Prisoner" are merely "Prishchepa" and "Konkin." Morison also insists on Anglicizing Russian names, as in "Sandy the Christ" (for "Sasha") and "The Life and Adventures of Matthew Pavlichenko" (for "Matvei"). Since this is the only translation with which most readers are familiar, however, I have retained his titles here. The presently out-of-print version by Andrew MacAndrew (*Lyubka the Cossack and Other Stories* [New York: American Library, 1963]) and the new translation by David McDuff (*Collected Stories* [New York: Penguin, 1995]) address these shortcomings (although especially MacAndrew adds distortions of his own; see n. 58 below).

43. Nils Åke Nilsson, "Isaak Babel's 'Perechod čerez Zbruč," *Scando-Slavica* 23 (1977): 65; Marc Schreurs, *Procedures of Montage in Isaak Babel's* Red Cavalry (Amsterdam: Rodopi, 1989), 175. Incidentally, the Russians crossed the Nieman in this war as well, but now it was in retreat from the Poles, who won a major victory on that river.

44. Gareth Williams, "The Rhetoric of Revolution in Babel's *Konarmija*," *Russian Literature* 15, 3 (1984): 283. It has even been suggested that Vardin was the ghostwriter of Budennyi's attack on Babel (Alice Stone Nakhimov-

sky, *Russian-Jewish Literature and Identity* (Baltimore: The Johns Hopkins University Press, 1992), 230, n. 38.

45. Schreurs, *Procedures of Montage*, 102–3.

46. "Pobol'she takikh Trunovykh!" (More such Trunovs!), *Sochineniia*, vol. 1, 202.

47. Davies, "'Konarmiya' Stories," 852. Gareth Williams makes the interesting observation ("The Rhetoric of Revolution," 293) that on the same page of *The Red Cavalryman* as Babel's obituary of Trunov was a description of the shooting down of two enemy aircraft by soldiers in the First Cavalry. This real-life montage is surely what gave Babel the idea of including the episode in the story.

48. See Gary L. Browning, "Russian Ornamental Prose," *Slavic and East European Journal* 23, 3 (Fall 1979): 346–53.

49. Isaak Babel', *Sochineniia* vol. 2, 373, 378.

50. Morison ignores this parallelism almost completely, and he and MacAndrew both mistranslate Volhynia as a river, when in fact it is a region. McDuff's "the quiet Volyn" seems to perpetuate the error.

51. Carol Luplow, *Isaac Babel's Red Cavalry* (Ann Arbor, 1982), 99–100.

52. On the relationship between especially Sergei Eisenstein's theory of montage and literature, see Schreurs, *Procedures of Montage*, 1–36.

53. See Williams, "The Rhetoric of Revolution," 279–98.

54. The Morison translation (42) obscures this connection. "Sacred" (or at least "special" – *sokrovennyi*) crockery becomes alien "occult" crockery, and the narrator is made to seem an ignorant Christian when he says that the Jews celebrate Easter rather than Passover. Corrected by MacAndrew and McDuff.

55. See Schreurs, *Procedures of Montage*, 46, and Jan van der Eng, "Types of Inner Tales in *Red Cavalry*," *Text and Context* (Stockholm: Almquist and Wiksell, 1987), 128–38.

56. For more detailed analyses of "Crossing into Poland," see Schreurs, *Procedures of Montage*, 171–99; Nilsson, "Isaak Babel's *Perechod čerez Zbruč*," 63–71; and Richard Young, "Theme in Fictional Literature: A Way into Complexity," *Language and Style* 13, 3 (1980): 61–71.

57. On the question of genre, see Jan van der Eng, "Red Cavalry: A Novel of Stories," *Russian Literature* 33 (1993): 249–64; Agnes Gereben, "Über die Kohärenz einer epischen Gattung," *Studia Slavica Academiae Scientarum Hungaricae* 27 (1981): 213–28; Agnes Gereben, "Some Aspects of

Narration in the Composition of Cycles of Short Stories," *Studia Slavica Academiae Scientarum Hungaricae* 28 (1982): 333–47; Agnes Gereben, "The Syntactics of Cycles of Short Stories," *Essays in Poetics* 11, 1 (1986): 44–75; Louis Iribarne, "Babel's *Red Cavalry* as a Baroque Novel," *Contemporary Literature* 14, 1 (1973): 58–77; Erzhebet Kaman, "Kompozitsiia knigi rasskazov I. Babelia 'Konarmiia,'" *Studia Slavica Academiae Scientarum Hungaricae* 25 (1979): 207–15; N. I. Khimukhina, "O zhanrovoi spetsifike 'Konarmii' I. Babelia," *Vestnik Moskovskogo universiteta*, seriia 9, *Filologiia*, 3 (1991): 26–32; David Lowe, "A Generic Approach to Babel's *Red Cavalry*," *Modern Fiction Studies* 28, 1 (Spring 1982): 69–78; R. Ross, "The Unity of Babel's *Konarmija*," *South Central Bulletin* 41, 4 (1981): 114–19. The use of the words *collection* and *cycle* here is for convenience and does not imply any rigorous generic classification.

58. Babel', *Sochineniia*, vol. 1, 238. MacAndrew evidently disagrees with the author, since he treats the stories as disjointed fragments when he takes the liberty of rearranging them in what he feels is their "proper" chronological and narrative order.

59. Babel', *Sochineniia*, vol. 1, 244.

60. Dmitrii Furmanov, *Sobranie sochinenii v chetyrekh tomakh*, vol. 4 (Moscow, 1961), 340.

61. James Falen, *Isaac Babel: Russian Master of the Short Story* (Knoxville, Tenn., 1974), 123–24. On nature imagery, especially the sun and the moon, see also Gareth Williams, "Two Leitmotifs in Babel's *Konarmija*," *Die Welt der Slaven* 17, 2 (1972): 308–17.

62. See Jan van Baak, *The Place of Space in Narration. A Semiotic Approach to the Problem of Literary Space. With an Analysis of the Role of Space in I. E. Babel's Konarmija* (Amsterdam: Rodopi, 1983), 150–51.

63. The English translation omits the name and patronymic. It should occur on page 80, after the line "he called out to me in despair." Corrected by McDuff (216).

64. Uralsk is incorrectly translated as "the Urals" (189). Corrected by McDuff (223).

65. See Robert Maguire, *Red Virgin Soil. Soviet Literature in the 1920s* (Ithaca: Cornell University Press, 1987), 327–29, 336–37.

66. E. A. Dobrenko makes a similar suggestion in a recent study of the structure of *Red Cavalry* ("Logika tsikla," in G. A. Belaia, E. A. Dobrenko, I. A. Esaulov, *"Konarmiia" Isaaka Babelia* [Moscow: Rossiiskii universitet,

1993], 33–101), but bases his division on the single criterion of individual identity versus identification with role identity (Dobrenko calls it "swarm consciousness" – *roevoe soznanie*). Although this yields some interesting results in many cases, in others it seems a bit thin, and I have preferred to use other criteria as well. Dobrenko does not posit a division at "The Cemetery at Kozin" and regards the final seven stories as codas completing various themes begun in the earlier ones.

67. Babel's use of the Polish word *kholop* to refer to the "destitute hordes" streaming into Poland produces several layers of ironic meaning. In Russian the word refers to serfs, bond slaves, especially in ancient Kievan Rus'. *Pesn' ob edinenii vsekh kholopov* (the song of the uniting of all the serfs) is of course a paraphrase of "The International." The modern meaning of the word is something like "obsequious lackey," and here it also echoes the Polish word *chłopy* (peasants) to which it is related, so that the final image is at best rather unproletarian.

68. See, in particular, Patricia Carden, *The Art of Isaac Babel* (Ithaca: Cornell University Press, 1972), 133–51; Falen, *Isaac Babel*, 180–87; and I. A. Esaulov, "Eticheskoe i esteticheskoe v rasskaze 'Pan Apolek,'" in G. A. Belaia et al., *"Konarmiia" Isaaka Babelia*, 102–16.

69. Falen, *Isaac Babel*, 186.

70. On Mikhail Bakhtin's notion of carnival, see especially his *Rabelais and His World* (Bloomington: Indiana Universeity Press, 1968).

71. Falen, *Isaac Babel*, 186–87.

72. A similar reevaluation of the aestheticist position is suggested in a later story as well. See Charles Rougle, "Art and the Artist in Babel's 'Guy de Maupassant,'" *Russian Review* 48, 2 (April 1989): 171–80.

73. See Martin Klotz, "Poetry of the Present: Isaac Babel's *Red Cavalry*," *Slavic and East European Journal* 18, 2 (1974): 160–69.

74. This is a common theme in Babel's earlier work (see Carden, *The Art of Isaac Babel*, 67–68) and runs through the works of other assimilated Jewish writers as well, particularly Eduard Bagritskii and Osip Mandel'shtam (see Nakhimovsky, *Russian-Jewish Literature and Identity*, 20–28).

75. For detailed analyses of this story, see Joe Andrew, "Babel's 'My First Goose,'" in *The Structural Analysis of Russian Narrative Fiction*, edited and with an introduction by J. Andrew (Keele: Essays in Poetics Publication No. 1, 1982), 64–81, and Yuri K. Shcheglov, "Some Themes and Archetypes in Babel's *Red Cavalry*, *Slavic Review* 53, 3 (Fall 1994): 653–70.

76. Ad de Vries, *Dictionary of Symbols and Imagery* (Amsterdam: North Holland, 1976), 41–42, 255–57.

77. Babel published a story entitled "Grishchuk" (*Sochineniia*, vol. 1, 436) but never included it in any of the editions of *Red Cavalry*.

78. For a detailed analysis of the structure and semiotics of this story, see Joost van der Baak, "Isaak Babel's 'Cemetery at Kozin,'" *Canadian Slavonic Papers* 36, 1–2 (March–June 1994): 69–87.

79. On the notion of cyclical time in *Red Cavalry*, see Falen, *Isaac Babel*, 172–73. In his diary entry of 18 July Babel noted of the cemetery: "A Jewish cemetery . . . it has seen Khmel'nitskii, now Budennyi, the unfortunate Jewish population; all is repeating, now this story – Poles – Cossacks – Jews – is repeating with astonishing accuracy; what's new is Communism" (Babel', *Sochineniia*, vol. 1, 378–79). See the expression of similar sentiments in the entries of 7 and 10 August.

80. Carden, *The Art of Isaac Babel*, 117.

81. Judith Deutsch Kornblatt, *The Cossack Hero in Russian Literature* (Madison, Wis.: University of Wisconsin Press, 1992), 122–25.

82. F. A. Brokgauz and I. A. Efron, *Entsiklopedicheskii slovar'* (St. Petersburg: Semenovskaia Tipografica, 1904), vol. 3, pt. 2, 527–28.

83. "Galin" was the original title of the story.

84. Falen, *Isaac Babel*, 95.

85. References to Trotskii were deleted in all but the 1926 edition of *Red Cavalry*. *Sochineniia* has restored them.

86. Schreurs, *Procedures of Montage*, 114–15.

87. The Morison translation misses this nuance, translating "zver'" – (wild) animal – as "the very devil." McDuff corrects it (191).

88. See Avins, "Kinship and Concealment," 707–8.

89. Alan Reid, "Isaak Babel's *Konarmiia*: Meanings and Endings," *Canadian Slavonic Papers* 33, 2 (June 1991): 142.

90. Avins, "Kinship and Concealment," 704–5.

91. Simon Markish, "Russko-evreiskaia literatura i Isaak Babel'," in Isaak Babel', *Detstvo i drugie rasskazy* (Jerusalem: Biblioteka-Aliia, 1989), 333; see also Dobrenko, "Logika tsikla," 93.

92. Avins, "Kinship and Concealment," 708.

93. Carden, *The Art of Isaac Babel*, 105–6.

94. Falen, *Isaac Babel*, 158–59; Nakhimovsky, *Russian-Jewish Literature and Identity*, 96–97.

95. The Morison translation – "I was there beside my brother" – completely obscures this possible connection. MacAndrew and McDuff are more literal.

96. Luplow, *Isaac Babel's* Red Cavalry, 112.

97. Klotz, "The Poetry of the Present," 169.

98. Falen, *Isaac Babel*, 199.

99. Reid, "Isaak Babel's *Konarmiia*, 149.

II   CRITICISM

Paradox and the Search for Value in Babel's *Red Cavalry*

CAROL LUPLOW

In *Red Cavalry* (*Konarmiia*, 1923–26) Isaak Babel grapples with major ethical, philosophical, and historical problems posed by the revolution and civil war. He questions, for example, whether significant changes can be effected by acting according to traditional humanist values; whether, if they cannot, violence is a justifiable means to attaining humanistic aims; whether violent means can achieve such aims or must inevitably pervert them. However, such historical concerns serve primarily to raise issues of broader scope. *Red Cavalry* centers on the exploration and evaluation of two radically different approaches to reality, ways of life, and value systems. Lionel Trilling calls these poles the way of violence and the way of peace.[1] Stanley Edgar Hyman states that the cycle further explores the conflict between "culture and nature, or art and the life of action, or freedom and necessity, or any philosophic phrasing of the Darwinian conflict between life in a moral order alienated from nature and natural law, and life in a natural order antecedent to morality."[2] At the core of all these polarities lies the basic opposition between the physical and spiritual-intellectual poles of reality and human nature.

These issues are explored primarily through the point of view and experiences of the narrator, who, along with the author, searches throughout the cycle for a viable value system. Though author and narrator are not identical, and the author often treats ironically the actions and attitudes of the narrator, they share the basic vision of the nature of reality that informs the cycle, a vision that complicates and hinders the search for value. Reality and human nature, in their view, consist of polar opposites that occur in different phenomena or paradoxically exist within one phenomenon or person. The world of man consists of antithetical and irreconcilable ways of life based on conflicting, incompatible value systems.

This vision of polarity and paradox is central to the worldview of *Red Cavalry* and dominates every level of the cycle – thematic, structural, narrative, and stylistic. Especially interesting is the thematic level. Within the primary opposition between the physical and the spiritual-intellectual poles of human nature, the cycle is dominated by a thematics of opposition which juxtaposes the past with the present, peace with violence, Jew with Cossack, humanist tradition with revolutionary change, the civilized with the primitive, and the rational with the irrational. Moreover, individual stories center on specific conflicts and polarities in theme and character. Not only does reality consist of polar opposites, but each pole may contain within itself paradoxical polarities or incongruities. Often, as a result, the very features that make a way of life, value system, or character admirable and compelling have inherent in them the qualities that make them unacceptable or nonviable. Thus, although *Red Cavalry* is seriously concerned with the search for value, its vision of reality leaves the issues of value so entangled in paradoxes that a final resolution of the search is impossible.[3]

This conflict between paradoxical vision and the search for value is developed in large part through the juxtaposition of two character groups – the Cossacks and the religious characters. The Cossacks represent the revolution, but more important, as semiliterate, crude professional soldiers they represent the way of violence, elemental man, the primitive, irrational, physical pole of human nature. The religious characters, who reject or stand to the side of the revolution, represent the way of peace and compassion, humanist, civilized, rational man, the spiritual and intellectual poles of human nature.

This clash between modes of existence and poles of human nature is perceived and experienced most fully by the narrator, Lyutov. A

Jewish intellectual serving among the Cossacks, he is torn between incompatible impulses and desires. He vacillates between the two radically different worlds as he tries to define his attitude toward them and find a place for himself. His attempts to resolve this conflict are complicated not only by his view of the paradoxical nature of reality but also by his romantic, aesthetic sensibilities, which sometimes conflict with his moral concerns, and by his psychological dilemmas. As a Jew he is torn between the world of his heritage and the modern world, between humanism and revolutionary values. As an intellectual, he is hyperconscious, prone to a rational search for design and the creation of a value system. But in his recognition of the complex, multifaceted nature of reality and man he finds that they will not fit into any pattern or system. He thus cannot unreservedly believe in or act for any cause. It is through his experiences and dilemmas, then, that the complexities of the paradoxical vision and the impasse in the search for value are most fully depicted.

The narrator's attitude toward the Cossacks is formed by both aesthetic and moral concerns. He has a romantic fascination, admiration, and even envy of the Cossacks and their way of life. They embody for him physical beauty, sensuality, prowess, vitality, and strength of body and will. They are courageous and daring, decisive and capable of immediate, direct action. They represent natural simplicity and the free expression of the elemental, instinctual life. In his attitude toward them the narrator is prey to what Trilling calls a "fantasy of personal animal grace," a "glory of conscienceless self-assertion, a sensual freedom" (29). The narrator succumbs to the romantic "fantasy of the noble savage," a fantasy that represents "the truth of the body, the truth of full sexuality, the truth of open aggressiveness" (18). He is fascinated by the "mysterious and elemental challenge of direct physical involvement in experience,"[4] a challenge he takes up but cannot meet. Ideal Cossack figures, sensually handsome, clothed in an operatic splendor of dress and gesture, in command of every situation, appear throughout the cycle. The most vivid of these are Savitsky in "My First Goose" ("Moi pervyi gus'") and Dyakov in "The Remount Officer" ("Nachal'nik konzapasa"), but many other stories depict the daring and heroism of the Cossacks. By his frequent use of epic themes and devices Babel often endows the Cossacks with an aura of epic heroism.[5]

Although the narrator thus romanticizes the Cossacks, his admiration and infatuation are qualified by his moral concerns, which arise from his realization that another basic and inescapable aspect of the Cossacks' physical nature is a strong impulse toward violence. Violence is not only the necessary means of implementing the revolution but is an integral part of the Cossacks' character and way of life, of the elemental physical pole which they embody. The narrator's major dilemma in relation to the Cossacks centers on how to come to terms with this fact. At times the narrator succumbs to a "mystique of violence" and romanticizes the ability of the Cossacks to be violent not only without inhibition but with flair and bravado. He accepts their violence as the ultimate expression of their physicality.

The narrator finds violence most acceptable when it is expressed in heroic action or motivated by revolutionary fervor and a sense of revolutionary justice. But the Cossacks' verbal adherence to the ideals of the revolution is actually of minor significance to him. The Cossacks' statements of support for the revolution occur only occasionally and are generally qualified by irony. They reveal the Cossacks' political naivete and their personal use of political slogans. In "The Story of a Horse" ("Istoriia odnoi loshadi"), for example, Khlebnikov writes a letter in which he affirms that "the Communist Party was founded, the way I see it, for joy and steadfast justice without limit and is also supposed to look out for the small fry."[6] But this statement of revolutionary ideals is made to support his personal claim to a horse. More important, the Cossacks' vociferous support of revolutionary justice is generally overshadowed by personal motives for violence, particularly vengeance. Although their violence is occasionally directed against the enemies of the revolution, as in "Squadron Commander Trunov" ("Eskadronnyi Trunov"), in which Trunov kills white prisoners, it is most often directed against enemies of the Cossacks, one's comrades, or oneself.

The man who defends violence most eloquently is Balmashev, who, in "Salt" ("Sol'"), demands revenge on an "enemy" who has insulted the revolution, his comrades, and himself. He has allowed a woman with her infant onto a crowded troop train and persuaded his soldiers not to touch her in accordance with revolutionary principle, which demands respect for motherhood and the baby, for whose future the revolution is being waged. His act is thus motivated by both "revolutionary consciousness" and compassion. When he discovers that the "infant" is a bag of smuggled salt, he argues with impassioned rhetoric that the woman has so brazenly insulted motherhood, the revolution, the future, the suffering people, Russia, and his comrades that the only possible retribution is death:

> And I admit straight off that I threw this citizenness off the moving train down the embankment, but she, crude hussy, just sat there, flapped her skirts, and went her vile way. And I, seeing this unharmable woman, and unspeakable Russia about her, and the peasants' fields without grain, and the violated girls, and my comrades, lots of who goes to the front and few comes back, I wanted to jump off the train and either make an end to myself or her. . . . So I yanked my trusty rifle off the wall and wiped this shame off the face of the working land and the republic. (93)

Aspects of Balmashev's character revealed earlier in the story – his protectiveness toward the woman, his loyalty to the principles of the revolution, his sensitive lyrical evocation of night and homesickness – emphasize the paradoxical contrast between Balmashev's initial compassion and subsequent ruthlessness, pulling the reader between sympathetic understanding and moral outrage.

In "After the Battle" ("Posle boia") Akinfiev reveals a similar dual motivation for violence, though the personal dominates. His hysterical outbursts indicate that he considers the narrator a traitor for going into battle with an unloaded gun because he cannot defend his comrades and because he shows that he "respects God," thereby betraying a major principle of the revolution. Furthermore, in not defending himself, he has displayed personal weakness, a contemptible and unforgivable sin in the Cossack code. And in "Two Ivans" ("Ivany") Akinfiev, with an emotional intensity equal to that of Balmashev, justifies his torture of Aggev, who pretends to be deaf in order to avoid fighting, by pointing to the common danger against which all must fight:

> I'd like to know if it's proper for us or not proper that when the enemy is unspeakably tormenting us, when the enemy is knocking hell out of us, when he hangs like a weight on our legs and binds our arms like snakes, is it proper for us to plug up our ears at this fatal hour? (115)

The validity of Akinfiev's rage is in part supported in the story by the image of Aggev, which suggests cowardice and weakness.

The Cossacks often identify a personal wrong with a social wrong that the revolution is seeking to rectify. But as Patricia Carden argues, even purely personal revenge is motivated by a search for justice or a desire to protest against injustice or a cruel fate (97). Thus "the most despicable acts have a kind of virtue when seen as protests against that fate, as assertions of the human spirit" (123).[7] In "The Life of Pavlichenko" ("Zhizneopisanie Pavlichenki, Matveia Rodionycha"), for example, the hero equates his personal revenge with revolutionary justice. He justifies his murder of his former master Nikitinsky as a revolutionary act by "reading" him a "letter" from Lenin that gives him carte blanche "in the name of the people . . . and for the establishment of the future bright life . . . to deprive various people of their life in accords with his discretion" (75). This letter, however, is in part a parody of the concept of revolutionary justice, for it reveals the Cossacks' belief that they have the right to kill according to their personal interpretation of the revolution and their equation of personal with revolutionary concerns.

But one cannot deny Pavlichenko's compelling personal reasons for seeking revenge. The first half of the story dramatizes Nikitinsky's humiliation of him. When Pavlichenko goes to confront his master about the latter's affair with his wife, Nikitinsky makes him wait in the doorway an hour unnoticed, then abuses him verbally, forces him to his knees, and slaps his face. The depth of Pavlichenko's humiliation is revealed in the second half of the story when he returns during the civil war and meets a group of landowners, who question him:

> "Comrade Pavlichenko, you, it seems, have galloped here from afar, and your face is covered all over with dirt. We, the local power, are terrified by such a face – why is that?"
>
> "That's because," I answer, "you local cold-blooded power, that's because on my face one cheek has been burning for five years; it burns in the trenches, it burns before women, it'll burn at the Last Judgment. At the Last Judgment." (75)

When Nikitinsky tries to buy Pavlichenko off, the latter replies:

> "And what about my cheek? What am I supposed to do about it," I says to him, "what's to be done about my cheek, my good friend and brother?" (76)

And Pavlichenko stamps Nikitinsky to death "an hour or more" to avenge his humiliated spirit and reestablish his self-esteem.

In "Afonka Bida" Afonka terrorizes an entire region to avenge the death of his horse in battle, an act that seems at first far in excess of the wrong done him. But two brief scenes in the story provide dramatic justification, as they establish the overwhelming magnitude of his grief and his loss: his hysterical lament and a brief conversation between two comrades:

> "He brought the horse from home," said the long-mustached Bitsenko. "Where's he to find another horse like that?"
>
> "A horse is a friend," replied Orlov.
>
> "A horse is a father," sighed Bitsenko, "he saves your life a million times over. Without a horse Bida's done for." (100–101)

Carden's interpretation of the Cossacks as seekers of justice and dignity is thus valid for many stories, but it does not fully explain all instances of violence. Although Carden recognizes the qualifications and ambiguity in the depiction of the Cossacks, their negative side, her emphasis on the clear dominance of a positive heroic image of the Cossacks (and other characters) over the various means of qualifying this image slights the complexity of vision in the cycle and the ambiguity to which it leads. The acceptance of violence is always qualified at least in part by irony, yet the rejection of violence is equally qualified. As the full dimensions of the Cossacks and the physical pole are revealed, it becomes impossible to take a decisive stand for or against them.

In the course of *Red Cavalry* the admiration and justification of the Cossacks are subjected to major moral qualifications through the narrator's reactions, judgments, and deeds, through irony, through a pervasive negative view of war, and through their juxtaposition to the religious characters. The narrator's attitude toward the Cossacks' violence is ambiguous and inconsistent. Sometimes he condones violence and courts acceptance by them, as in "My First Goose" and "After the Battle." At other times he is repulsed and spurns them, as in "Two Ivans" and "The Road to Brody" ("Put' v Brody"). He generally sees his revulsion as a weakness, but it frequently stands as a condemnation of violence. He easily defends bloodshed in abstract conversation, as in "Gedali," but when directly confronted with violence he recoils and calls for compassion. The Cossacks' ready use and justification of violence is then juxtaposed to the narrator's qualified or complete rejection. In "The Road to Brody," for example, he symbolically connects and sadly laments the destruction of the bees, whose hives the starving Cossacks plunder, and the massacre at Brody, and he deplores "the chronicle of our everyday crimes." Yet the narrator's horror at the violence is countered by the Cossacks' hunger, which necessitates the destruction of the bees, and by Afonka's assertion that violence is necessary for the creation of a better future: "The bee's gotta understand. The bee'll have to endure. It's for it too we're messing about here" (56). The story thus presents two irreconcilable points of view, stated with equal feeling and certitude. In "Squadron Commander Trunov," too, Lyutov is torn between moral outrage at Trunov's killing of the prisoners and admiration for Trunov's daring battle with the planes and brave self-sacrifice. But he never vindicates the execution of the Whites, he only admits that he has no right to judge, perhaps because he can neither fully understand nor emulate Trunov, perhaps because he recognizes that two antithetical truths paradoxically coexist in Trunov.

In some stories, though, the sense of oppression before violence dominates. In "Two Ivans" Akinfiev's justification of his torture of Aggev and the sense of Aggev's weakness are overshadowed by the narrator's revulsion and depression, which are communicated primarily through imagery. At nightfall, after a day spent picking up wounded men, the narrator finds himself exhausted and alone by a ruined hut. The whole universe seems engulfed in the holocaust of war:

> Night flew toward me on her swift steeds. The howling of cats resounded through the universe. On the earth, an earth encircled by screams, the roads faded out of sight. Stars crawled out of night's cool belly, and abandoned villages flared up over the horizon. (116)

The narrator accidentally urinates on the face of a corpse. He wipes the urine off and walks away burdened by depression. Images of defilement and decay symbolize the moral degradation of the war: a rotting ox foot on which the men feed, Akinfiev's venereal disease and his comrades' crude jokes about it, and a field full of human excrement. The sense of defilement is summed up in the comment of an old man who sees the narrator vainly looking for a place to rest in the field: "Humans we calls ourselves, but we fouls things up worse than jackals. The earth is shamed" (118). And the narrator at the end of the story walks away overcome by "weakness and despair."

Even when the Cossacks narrate their own stories, irony and black humor undercut the pathos of their self-justifying speech. In "Salt" the humor of Balmashev's garbled speech and the irony of his outrageous statement that soldiers are forced by loneliness to rape girls and of his final oath "to deal mercilessly with all those traitors that drag us into the pit and want to turn the stream back and bestrew Russia with corpses and dead grass" (93) temper the pathos of his laments for Russia and his outraged sense of justice.

When Pavlichenko describes how he stamped his master to death, he explains:

> And then I stomped on my master Nikitinsky. I stomped on him for an hour or more, and during that time I got to know life completely. With a shot, I tell you, all you can do is get rid of a man. A shot is a mercy to him and a damned easy way out for yourself; with a shot you don't get to the soul, to where it is in a man and how it shows itself. But I make it a habit not to spare myself. I make it a habit to stomp on my enemy for an hour or more, I want to get to know life, what it's like among us. (76)

This equation of killing with knowledge of life and torture with getting to understand a man underscores the fact that violence is at the core of the physical approach to reality. Yet the horror of this final statement does not totally undercut the compelling motivation for Pavlichenko's revenge. The story thus presents two points of view – incompatible, yet seemingly of equal validity.

Violence is at times implicitly condemned by such gratuitous acts as the murder of the old Jew in "Crossing the Zbruch" ("Perekhod cherez Zbruch"), the slitting of the old man's throat in "Berestechko," the blinding of Gedali in "Gedali," and the massacre of the Jews in "Zamość" ("Zamost'e"). And even motivated violence is at times inordinately brutal, as in "Two Ivans," "Afonka Bida," and "The Life of Pavlichenko."

The narrator's, and author's, inability to fully accept the Cossack way, then, results from the recognition of the essential flaw inherent in the physical pole of human nature. While physicality is in many respects compelling and desirable, inherent in it are violence and unrestrained passion. Violence itself, though at times seemingly justified and necessary, inevitably erupts into acts of wanton destruction and senseless brutality. The use of violence as a means seems to lead inevitably to violence as the way of action, the way of dealing with reality and asserting one's will.

The two-sided nature of violence is illustrated well in the character of Afonka Bida. In "The Road to Brody" Afonka suggests that violence is necessary to create the new future, and so rejects the compassion affirmed in the tale of Christ and the bees. In "Afonka Bida" his revenge for the death of his horse is motivated, but in the first part of the story he joyfully participates in the senseless whipping of peasant soldiers. When the narrator protests and asks for the reason for this, Afonka flippantly replies, "For laughs. . . . For laughs" (99). In "In St. Valentine's Church" ("U sviatogo Valenta"), after returning with a new horse Bida senselessly vandalizes the church. In "The Death of Dolgushov" ("Smert' Dolgushova") Bida is able to kill Dolgushov without hestitation, an act of mercy, to spare him torture at the hands of the Poles, whereas the humanist narrator cannot. But in his rage at the narrator, Bida almost kills him too. The Cossack can commit violence for a good end, out of rage, from grief, for fun, to attain knowledge, or for any other reason. The Cossack way leads to glorification of violence for its own sake. In "My First Goose," for example, the condition of the narrator's acceptance by the Cossacks is the senseless violation of a weak, innocent person, and in "The Life of Pavlichenko" the hero sings a paean to the violence of the revolution and laments its end.

The narrator's romantic admiration of the Cossacks is further questioned by the irony directed at his attempts to join their world and himself engage in violent action. In "My First Goose" his ludicrous "murder" of an old woman's goose in lieu of raping the "purest little lady," and his remorse even at this act, seem to deflate the romantic image of the Cossack. In his attempt to emulate them he has reduced their epic grandeur and passion to ludicrous comedy. Thus one may question whether his failure reflects on the Cossacks and their heroic image or reveals his debasement of that image. The Cossack image itself is lowered before the narrator commits his "murder," as the romantic Savitsky is superseded by the Cossack youth who flatulates to show his contempt for the narrator. The effect of low comedy is furthered by other base images in the story. The story, then, leaves the reader in a tangle of irresolvable ambiguities. The moral and aesthetic issues are too complex and multi-faceted to lead to a final stand. The story simply juxtaposes the romantic image of Savitsky with the low image of the youth, the grandeur of Savitsky with the ludicrous baseness of the narrator, the flamboyant hero with the despairing victim, the heroic violence that wins battles with the petty violence that seeks entertainment at the expense of the violated. The question of whether the narrator debases only himself, whether his actions reflect on those Cossacks who spur him on, or whether they reflect on the whole Cossack ethos is never decisively answered. And the larger issue of the consequences for a moral stand if heroic or justified violence does lead inevitably to base, senseless violence is likewise left unresolved, in this story and in the whole cycle.

In a number of stories the narrator is unable to act rightly with respect to either group of characters or code of action. In both "Zamość" and "The Song" ("Pesnia") he again violates helpless old women. In some situations the narrator's futile attempts to join the Cossack world are clear failures on his part. In "The Death of Dolgushov," where to kill is an act of compassion, the narrator is paralyzed by his humanist values, which have no validity in this situation. Thus, paradoxically, his failure to kill is a failure of compassion, as Afonka furiously accuses: "You four-eyes pity our brothers like a cat pities a mouse" (63). Afonka's harsh judgment, however, is tempered by the story's implicit condemnation of war and the distortion of values that it inevitably entails. The story is set against a background of all-pervading death, bullets greedily seeking human flesh, and Grishchuk's lament for the futile labors of women, who bear sons only to be killed in war. Similarly, the narrator's failure to help his comrades in "After the Battle" and his prayer for "the simplest of all abilities – the ability to kill a human being" (141) are in part countered by a strong sense in the story of the degradation of war. Thus among the Cossacks Lyutov is too weak and indecisive to fulfill his obligations to his comrades or to live fully by their code. But just as he at times believes in the Cossack way but when with them cannot live up to it, so at other times he believes in the compassion of the spiritual characters but does not himself act with compassion, and even violates the weak.

Red Cavalry in part chronicles the horrors of war. Images of its horrors provide a constant indirect commentary against war and the excesses of the physical pole. The opening story, "Crossing the Zbruch," depicts the entrance into a war world as a descent into a hell of destruction and desecration.[9] A beautiful, pure landscape yields, as the army crosses the river into Poland, to destructive chaos in which nature is crudely violated. This violation presages the revelation of the defilement of the Jewish family's home, the father's murder, and the narrator's spiritual desecration of the family by his insensitivity and contempt.

The horrors of war are depicted most often in the latter part of the cycle, as the narrator penetrates ever more deeply into a world of death, brutality, treachery, and desecration. This atmosphere is summed up in the narrator's lament over the endless war in "The Song" and in the wet, barren autumnal landscapes, marked by striking images of exhaustion and death, in "Zamość" and "After the Battle." The stories in the second half of the cycle focus often on cruel revenge and brutality, on deceit and treachery, as if the war had brought to the surface the worst elements in man's nature to rampage uncontrolled.

But although the Cossack way is subjected to strong moral qualifications with respect to their inherent violence, the narrator and author never lose their admiration for their positive qualities, never fully accept or reject them. As Trilling says: "For Babel it is not violence in itself that is at issue in relation to the Cossacks, but something else. . . . Rather he is drawn by what the violence goes along with, the boldness, the passionateness, the simplicity and directness – and the grace." But "Babel never for a moment forgets what the actualities of this savage glory are" (28–29).

The religious characters provide the antithesis to the Cossack way. They exert an attraction on the narrator as strong as that of the Cossacks, for they possess a spiritual beauty, strength, and passion commensurate with the positive physical attributes of the Cossacks.

But the narrator perceives major flaws in the religious characters, concomitant to their positive features, which lead to the same insolubly ambiguous attitudes toward them that he feels toward the Cossacks.

The humanist tradition to which the religious characters belong, in contrast to the Cossack way, affirms the nobility and worth of the individual, respects human life, values love, compassion, and peace, and treasures beauty, wisdom, and spirituality. The religious characters have the moral and spiritual virtues that the narrator values (sometimes in spite of himself) and that the Cossacks lack. But they lack the positive physical qualities that the narrator so admires in the Cossacks. The religious characters are puny, weak, and defective in body. These physical defects in part symbolize their otherworldly nature, but they also symbolize their isolation from and ineffectuality in dealing with the physical world. This duality in the spiritual pole is most fully depicted in the Jewish characters, and it is toward them that the narrator is most ambiguous.[10] Their tradition and values are deeply ingrained in him, and he must free himself from them in order to affirm the physical world.

Gedali embodies for the narrator the best and worst features of the Jewish world and the spiritual pole. In "Gedali" the old Jew contrasts two radically different kinds of revolution, and this antithesis epitomizes the difference between the two poles of reality. The narrator affirms the inevitability of violence in a revolution. But Gedali, who has been violated by both Poles and Cossacks and has seen how both destroy indiscriminately, with inexorable logic and emotional intensity argues that they are identical, that there must be a true revolution, a "sweet revolution" that affirms peace and compassion:

"But the Pole, kind sir, shot because he is the counterrevolution. You shoot because you are the revolution. But a revolution is pleasure. And pleasure does not like orphans in the house. Good deeds are done by good people. A revolution is the good deed of good people. But good people do not kill. That means that it is evil people who are making the revolution. But the Poles are also evil people. Then who is to tell Gedali which is the revolution and which the counterrevolution?" (47)

"The International . . . we know what the International is. But I want an International of good people. I want every soul to be registered and given first category rations. Here, soul, please eat, enjoy the pleasures of life." (48)

In "Gedali" the narrator reveals the compelling hold of his heritage as he searches for the Jewish community on a sabbath eve and depicts Gedali's moral and spiritual fervor. But he also rejects his heritage and defends the revolution. For him this tradition, embodied in the saintly, wise, but impotent and somewhat ludicrous old Gedali, is not a viable alternative to the Cossack way. Bent on otherworldly concerns and values, the Jewish world stands outside time and history, and remains unchanged through the ages. It cannot participate in or cope with the forces of change and renewal that are essential to life and history. Gedali lives alone with his "impossible dream" in a dead, deserted bazaar and keeps an antique shop filled with old, dead broken things. He is touched by the present only to be injured by it. The images of old age, decay, and death suggest that the Jewish world is itself moribund, a theme that continues in "The Rabbi" ("Rabbi").

"Gedali" centers on an irreconcilable paradox. Gedali is a passionate spokesman for life, joy, and an ideal future, but he is old, weak, and loyal to a moribund past. He may be a passionate dreamer and saint, but he is also an ineffectual victim. This combination of spiritual strength, passion, and beauty with physical impotence causes the narrator's ambiguous mixture of admiration and revulsion toward the Jewish figures and the spirituality they embody. Yet, paradoxically, the narrator, who has rejected the dead past, in "Gedali" speaks only for the bloodshed and destruction of the present: "It cannot help but shoot Gedali, . . . because it is the Revolution" (47) and "They feed it [the International] with gunpowder and spice it with the best blood" (48).

The Jewish settlements that the narrator visits in Poland are marked by this same ineffectuality and decay. In "Berestechko" he depicts most starkly the stagnation and squalor of the Jews:

> Berestechko stinks indissolubly to this very day, all the people reek with the stench of rotten herring. The place stinks in expectation of a new era, and instead of people, the faded outlines of frontier disasters walk its streets. (88)

Yet, as in "Gedali," the revolution is seen mainly as the bearer of death and destruction. It is merely the latest in an endless series of conquests, which are in large part responsible for the wretchedness of the oppressed Jewish settlements. But the narrator also sees in the shtetl Jews the same paradoxical combination of features that he saw in Gedali: spiritual passion and nobility as well as decay and degradation. This duality and the narrator's ambiguous attitude toward it are lyrically evoked in the picture of the Galician Jews in "Discourse on the Tachanka" ("Uchenie O tachanke"):

> Lifeless little Jewish villages clung to the feet of Polish noblemen's estates. On brick fences glimmered a vatic peacock, dispassionate vision in azure expanses. Hidden away behind sprawling hovels, a synagogue, eyeless, pockmarked, round as a Hasidic hat, squatted on the destitute land. Narrow-shouldered Jews stood mournfully at the crossroads. . . . One cannot compare with [the southern Jews] the bitter arrogance of these long bony backs, these tragic yellow beards. In these passionate features, carved out in agony, there is neither fat nor warm coursing blood. The movements of the Galician and Volhynian Jews are controlled and jerky, offensive to the taste, but the strength of their sorrow is suffused with a twilight grandeur, and their clandestine contempt for the Polish nobleman is boundless. Watching them, I understood the searing history of this region, the tales of Talmudic scholars who ran taverns, of rabbis who practiced usury, of girls who were raped by Polish soldiers and over whom Polish magnates duelled. (60)

In "The Rabbi's Son" ("Syn Rabbi"), originally the last story in the cycle, the fundamental incompatibility of the two worlds of *Red Cavalry* is embodied in the contrast of objects in the son's trunk. The things that represent the Jewish world, the spiritual realm, bespeak poetry, beauty, faith, and love: books of poetry, a silken portrait of the theologian-philosopher Maimonides, a lock of a woman's hair, ancient Hebrew verses, the "Song of Songs," and phylacteries. The things that represent the communist world, the physical pole, suggest practicality, harshness, and violence: propaganda leaflets, a portrait of Lenin that highlights the "nodulous iron" of his skull, a book of resolutions of the Sixth Party Congress, revolver shells, and foot cloths. The flaws in each world, which are inextricably linked to their best qualities, remind the narrator again of his conflicts vis-à-vis the two worlds and the values they represent. And in this story, his ambiguous attitude toward both remains unresolved.

The narrator's hopes for a reconciliation of the two worlds and for the entrance of the Jewish world into the present rest on the rabbi's son. Ilya rejects his heritage by joining the Red Army. Furthermore, in his statement, "a mother in the Revolution is an episode" (146), he implicitly rejects Gedali's view of the mother, which gives a metaphoric statement of the spiritual outlook:

> Everything is mortal. Eternal life is granted only to the mother. Even when the mother is no longer alive she leaves her memory after her, which no one yet has dared defile. Memory of the mother nourishes in us compassion, just as the ocean, the boundless ocean nourishes the rivers which cleave the universe. (53)

In his heroic stand against the enemy Ilya has proved capable of decisive action and courage, but his success is incomplete. His impasse in his attempt to reject the past and enter the present is revealed by the paradoxical array of things in his trunk. The narrator's reaction when he finds them – "They fell on me like a melancholy and meager rain" (146) – perhaps indicates his recognition that the two worlds are antithetic and irreconcilable. The narrator's impasse is compounded by his recognition that although the one world is filled with poetry, wisdom, and beauty, it is moribund, whereas the other world, though vital and aimed toward a better futue, brings only destruction and death.[11]

Ilya's possible failure to bring the two worlds together is further suggested by the futility of his heroic effort to save a battle, his arrival at the train emaciated, half-naked and dying, and his death and burial at a "forgotten station" (see also Falen, 159). There is at least a partial triumph and heroism in his break from the past and his self-sacrifice. Yet the question remains whether Ilya is destroyed by his ties to his heritage or by the senseless destruction of the revolution. Is his death, then, a tragic triumph, the inevitable failure of a Jew to deal with physical reality, or is it the failure of the revolution, the physical world, that brings about his death? Or does the story simply reveal the tragic irreconcilability of the two poles?

The narrator describes the Christian figures more positively than the Jewish, perhaps because he is free of intense emotional involvement. The basic spiritual values of the Christian tradition, though debased and distorted by the Church, continue in such solitary figures as Pan Apolek and Sashka the Christ. Apolek preaches through his paintings the divinity of the ordinary individual with all his flaws, in all his lowness (see also Carden, 133–40). He expresses this vision by painting the local peasants as saints, the holy family, Magi, and church fathers. The most vivid examples are the paintings of a crippled convert and social outcast as the apostle Paul and a homeless, half-witted girl with many illegitimate children as Mary Magdalene. Apolek's "blasphemous" legend of Christ and Deborah reveals the divine nature of the "low" physical act when consummated out of compassion. The contrast between the "heretic" Apolek's view of man and the Church's view, stated in a dialog between Church officials who have come to denounce him and the common people who defend him, reveals further that Apolek teaches men a higher view of themselves and returns to them their dignity and self-esteem.

"Your Holiness," said the lame Vitold, fence and cemetery watchman, to the vicar. . . . And is there not more truth in the pictures of Pan Apolek, who satisfies our pride, than in your words, so full of abuse and lordly wrath?" (39)

Apolek's tenacious thirty-year fight against the Church, the proliferation of his paintings in the villages, and the people's loyalty to him prove the strength of his message. Even the narrator is led to a new perception of people and inspired to renounce his hatred and contempt for the "curs and swine of humanity."

The image of Christ in Apolek's tale is realized in the figure of Sashka the Christ, who embodies in his syphilis and saintliness the paradoxical union of the earthly and divine. Details in the story "Sashka the Christ" ("Sashka Christos") establish parallels between the biographies of Jesus and Sashka, who attains maturity and leaves home to begin his wanderings and ministry. It is through his physical impurity that Sashka attains sainthood, for he uses his syphilis to coerce his father into letting him become a shepherd, in which role he leads his saintly life. In the people's perception, too, the paradoxical traits are linked as inextricable attributes of his saintliness:

He became renowned throughout the whole region for his openheartedness; he received from the villagers the nickname "Sashka the Christ" and he lived continuously as a shepherd until he was drafted. Old peasants, those who fared ill, would come out to the pasture to see him and wag their tongues. Womenfolk would come running to Sashka to recover from the senseless acts of their menfolk and did not get angry at Sashka, because of his love and because of his illness. (70–71)

And in "The Song" Sashka reenacts the union of the divine and the physical, echoing the tale of Christ and Deborah, as he lies with the landlady to console her in her misery.

This union of the earthly and divine, the physical and spiritual, approaches the ideal for which the narrator yearns. Yet the Christian characters, too, do not attain the ideal. They, like the Jewish figures, lack the physical attributes that the narrator admires in the Cossacks. Their physicality still lacks the strength, the open vitality and sensuality of the Cossacks. Like the Jewish figures, Apolek and Sashka stand on the periphery of events. The religious characters do not have the physical power or will to change the world or to defend themselves against the onslaught of the revolution and the Cossacks. They are artists and visionaries, not men of action. Their strength lies in their ability to offer transcendent moments of spiritual value, to provide consolation and love, and to restore to people their dignity and self-esteem. The paradoxical union of helplessness and power in the Christian figures is effectively symbolized in the image of Christ in "In St. Valentine's Church." Apolek's statue depicts Christ as a frightened, wounded victim fleeing his pursuers. But this view of Christ as ordinary man and helpless victim is offset by the powerful emotional effect the statue has on those who see it, as it moves the deacon and the narrator to bold acts of protest.

In *Red Cavalry* there seems at times to be an underlying pessimistic view of human nature and the human condition, a view that arises from the clash between the vision of paradox and the desire to find enduring value. There seems no way of bridging the gap between the physical and spiritual poles or of synthesizing the best of each. By the very nature of their spiritual passion, the religious characters divorce themselves from the physical world, from the beauty and vitality of the body, and prove ineffectual in dealing with reality. Nor can there be a reconciliation of the two concomitant aspects of the Cossack way. Their heroism, freedom, sensuality, and physical beauty are offset by the horrors of the mindless violence that is a corollary of their physical nature. Nor is there a reconciliation of the idealistic aims of the revolution with its brutal destructiveness. The Cossacks seem incapable of creating a "bright future" because they lack the transcending spiritual values by which to curb the elemental, irrational violent manifestations of their nature. Yet the religious characters cannot realize a "bright future" because they cannot assert their will toward change in the physical world.

But at other times *Red Cavalry* presents as equally valid Apolek's and Gedali's optimistic vision of the divinity and goodness of man, affirming this vision by depicting the beauty and heroism, the desire for justice, of both the Cossacks and religious characters.

Thus *Red Cavalry* maintains in precarious equilibrium the positive and negative features, both aesthetic and moral, of the physical and spiritual realms. It presents two irreconcilable truths, which carry within themselves irreconcilable polar opposites in paradoxical union. The narrator's duality is thus the dilemma of man faced with a paradoxical world in which irreconcilable polarities are at the foundation of existence and human nature. The complexity of experience and the paradoxical nature of reality make it impossible to find permanent, absolute order and value. *Red Cavalry* thereby remains in irresolvable tension, and the search for value ends in ambiguity and irresolution.

NOTES

1. Lionel Trilling, "Introduction" to Isaac Babel, *The Collected Stories*, translated by Walter Morison (Cleveland: World Publishing [Meridian Fiction], 1964), 14.

2. Stanley Edgar Hyman, "Identities of Isaac Babel: The Collected Stories of Isaac Babel," *The Hudson Review* 8 (1956): 622–23.

3. The complexity of *Red Cavalry* has led to markedly different interpretations of the cycle. My main disagreement is with the assumption that although Babel's attitude is complex and ambiguous, he nevertheless resolved the moral and philosophical issues with which he deals. The one exception is critics who deny that Babel has moral seriousness. R. W. Hallet states that Babel's "work seems almost totally lacking in moral seriousness" and that "he was primarily a superb stylist with a limited form and a limited range who regarded pure content as secondary" (*Isaac Babel* [Letchworth, Hertfordshire: Bradda Books, 1972], 133–36). Il'ia Erenburg states that Babel shares the humanist viewpoint represented by Gedali ("I. E. Babel'," in I Babel', *Konarmiia, Odesskie rasskazy, p'esy* [Moscow: GIkhL, 1957; rpt. Letchworth: Bradda Books, 1965] 18). A number of critics conclude that Babel justifies the violence of the Cossacks, though he is at times repelled by it, because he sees their acts as heroic strivings toward justice (personal or

revolutionary). I. Il'inskii contrasts codified law, the "law of the state," which the Cossacks reject, with "elemental law," "the law of life," a personal sense of justice, which they create and enforce in accordance with the conditions of their life and the revolutionary times ("Pravovye motivy v tvorchestve Babelia," *Krasnaia nov'*, no. 7 [1927]: 231–40). A. K. Voronskii states that Babel, though horrified by the cruelty of the Cossacks, sees as foremost and justifying the Cossacks the fact that they, as well as the religious characters, are all "seekers of justice" (*pravdo-iskateli*) who search for truth and justice in their own way ("I. Babel'," *Literaturnye tipy*, 2d ed. [Moscow: Krug, 1927; rpt. Ann Arbor, Mich.: University Microfilms, 1962], 67–76). This opinion is shared by L. Plotkin, but he sees Babel's attempts to justify the Cossacks as those of a petty-bourgeois intellectual who cannot accept the destructive violence of the revolution or the "blood, dirt, and cruelty of life." Babel therefore "romanticizes" and "idealizes" reality and the Cossacks in "petty-bourgeois humanist" moral terms, finding the Cossacks to be fighters for the abstract bourgeois-humanist moral ideals of justice and truth ("Tvorchestvo Babelia," *Oktiabr'*, no. 3 [1933]: 177–78). L. M. Poliak claims that *Red Cavalry* is "in essence an argument with Gedali, an affirmation of the right-ness and greatness of the revolution." Though Babel is horrified at cruelty, nevertheless "the entire book – and this is its contradictory nature – is a justification of necessary cruelty, cruelty in the name of justice, in the name of its future annihilation" ("I. E. Babel'," *Istorija russkoi sovetskoi literatury*, 4 vols. [Moscow: AN SSSR, 1967–71], vol. 1, 358–59). The best insights into this interpretation are by Patricia Carden, who brings greater philosophical depth to what is mainly political interpretation by the Soviet critics. She states that Babel portrays both Cossacks and religious characters as heroes (*The Art of Isaac Babel* [Ithaca: Cornell University Press, 1972], 101–32). For the Cossacks heroism is a physical standard, whereas for the religious char-acters it is a spiritual and ethical matter. But both strive for truth and justice. Though she has treated one side of the argument with insight and depth, she perhaps makes the case too one-sided and slights Babel the paradoxalist. Some Soviet critics find that though Babel showed a hatred of war and cruelty, he justified the cruelty and violence of the revolution as necessary to establish the new and better order. I. A. Smirin states that Babel, while depicting the contradictions in the Cossacks and the revolution, justified them in terms of their elemental beauty and heroism, their comradeship and unity, and their revolutionary fervor and ideas. They were "realizing the great historical mission of liberating mankind and bearing in their hands, crimson with blood, a higher justice, the future happy life." *Red Cavalry* shows "the threatening force, the turbulent band, the dashing Cossack *vol'nica* in the service of the revolution" ("Na puti k 'Konarmii' [Literaturnye iskaniia Babelia]," *Literaturnoe nasledstvo* 74 [1965]: 476–77). F. Levin agrees with Smirin's position (*I. Babel': ocherk tvorchestva* [Moscow: GIkhL, 1972], 84–103, 114–16). Thus Babel justifies the bloodshed and violence as necessary to "destroy the old world and create a new, better, bright future." Both Plotkin and Poliak emphasize Babel's acceptance of the goals of the revolution. Some critics emphasize the contradictions and ambiguities of *Red Cavalry* but still see a final resolution. Other Soviet critics state that Babel is caught in an irreconcilable conflict in which he justifies the revolution in the name of the future but cannot free himself from his humanist values to fully accept the inevitable cruelties of war. A. Z. Lezhnev stresses the conflict in Babel between his humane feelings and agony over cruelty and his depiction of the heroism of the Cossacks: "The justification of cruelty strangely and contradictorily resides with his non-acceptance of it. There is no way out of this contradiction" ("I. Babel'," *Sovremenniki: kriticheskie ocherki* [Moscow: Krug, 1927], 119–218). A. Makarov notes that the author, like Liutov, "is caught in a contradiction and cannot free himself from all of his old values," from his faulty "bourgeois humanism" ("Razgovor po povodu," *Znamia*, no. 4 [1958]: 195–96). Two American critics recognize the complexity and irresolvable ambiguities in *Red Cavalry* (Trilling, 14–17, 27–37; James E. Falen, *Isaac Babel: Russian Master of the Short Story* [Knoxville: University of Tennessee Press, 1974], 132–59). Their positions are given in greater detail in the text of this article. This article is an expansion of and further development of their position, an attempt to find the philosophical outlook at the base of Babel's vision, leading to his irresolvable ambiguity. The variety of opinions and interpretations of Babel is testament to the complexity and ambiguity of his vision. *Red Cavalry* defies definitive interpretation because there is no defined position – Babel's vision of the complexity and paradoxical nature of reality makes it impossible for him to take a decisive stand in relation to the problem of values, however earnest his search.

4. James Falen, "Isaac Babel: His Life and Art," Ph.D. dissertation, The University of Pennsylvania, 1970, 11.

5. In "The Brigade Commander" ("Kombrig dva"), Babel makes an epic hero of Kolesnikov, ending the story with a panegyric that ranks him with

other legendary heroes of the revolution. Many critics have pointed to Babel's use of epic themes, motifs, and devices. Although Babel at times uses them to endow characters and events with a heroic-epic aura, at other times he uses them in a mock-heroic manner to undercut by means of ironic contrast the ideal Cossack image with which the narrator is obsessed. For a list of some of Babel's epic motifs and devices and for the suggestion that they are used as travesty, see especially Victor Terras, "Line and Color: The Structure of I. Babel's Short Stories in *Red Cavalry*," *Studies in Short Fiction* 3 (1966), 144–50. Falen also discusses epic devices (119–24).

6. Isaak Babel', *Konarmiia. Odesskie rasskazy, p'esy*, 82. All quotes from Babel are taken from this edition. The translations are mine, though I am indebted to Walter Morison's translation of Isaac Babel, *The Collected Stories*.

7. Carden states: "The characters of *Red Cavalry* have in common the ability to protest. The protest may be treated ironically or seriously, but it is always present. It may be the verbal protest of Gedali, Khlebnikov, or the Jewish woman in 'Crossing the Zbruch.' It may be embodied in a work of art, as in Apolek's paintings, which protest the denigration of mankind, or in Sashka Khristos's songs, which protest against the injustice inherent in the universe. It may be embodied in an act of violence like the narrator's killing of the goose in 'My First Goose' or Matthew Pavlichenko's killing of his master. The characters of *Red Cavalry* have in common . . . their refusal to submit to their fates. . . . Whatever the characteristics of the individual figures, it is Babel's custom to show them as exceptional, as men who register their protest in the face of a cruel fate" (118). Carden concurs with Il'inskii, Voronskii, Plotkin, and Poliak.

8. Carden states: "Often the ostensible motive for destruction is revenge, but in every case Babel suggests a more serious goal, the attainment of extraordinary knowledge" (116). But she glosses over Babel's undercutting by various means of a serious acceptance of torture and murder as a path to knowledge.

9. The symbolic significance of the crossing of the river is discussed at length by Falen (137–41) and Louis H. Leiter ("A Reading of Isaac Babel's 'Crossing into Poland,'" *Studies in Short Fiction* 3 [1966], 199–206).

10. Falen has an excellent analysis of the narrator's ambiguous attitudes toward his Jewish heritage and the Jewish community (150–59).

11. Falen states: "(Liutov] is caught between two worlds, each of which fills him at times with horror or disgust. If he seeks among his army com-

rades to escape the suffering and deprivation of the closed old Jewish world, he collides with the harshness and cruelty of the Cossack way of life. The book is propelled forward through a recurring pattern of advance and retreat . . . of hope alternating with despair. . . . Whenever the narrator's sense of humanity is violated beyond endurance, he retreats to the Jewish ghetto, where he seeks a kind of companionship that the Cossacks cannot provide. He reemerges each time, it is true, but the pattern of withdrawal is recurrent" (149–50).

Babel's *Red Cavalry*: Epic and Pathos, History and Culture

MILTON EHRE

Isaak Babel's masterpiece of revolution and civil war, though a collection of short stories, is also a book shaped into an artistic whole by patterns of style and a central action or plot. Renato Poggioli detected two major stylistic strains in the work – the "epic-heroic" and the "pathetic" – an insight that criticism has yet to pursue.[1] Though much of *Red Cavalry* is devoted to genre sketches and anecdotes (many told in the speech of its characters, or *skaz*), the epic and pathetic modes function as polarities about which the diverse tales are organized. Each has its own language and clusters of imagery, and their interplay lends the work its distinctive shape and meanings.

The epic dominates. It is the mode of heroic action, running through the book like a straight line, interrupted and then resumed. Its subject is armies on the move, notably the warlike Cossacks who are changing the face of Eastern Europe. From the epic line, which has a relatively fixed character, digressive curves veer away to chart scenes and incidents viewed from the roads of war. These usually depict the two important cultures of the area – Catholic, aristocratic Poland and the Jewish Pale of Settlement – where the victims of war are to be found.[2] The epic and pathetic contrast is also a confrontation of history and culture.

By threading a plot through individual stories, Babel is able to span the divergent styles and subjects of his book. His plot brings a novelistic coherence to what otherwise would have remained a motley of sketches. *Red Cavalry* tells of the education into the ways of the world of the narrator, a sensitive Jewish intellectual named Lyutov (the fierce one), incongruously dropped among the truly fierce and often rabidly anti-Semitic Cossacks.[3] Lyutov's story proceeds through his painful initiation into the Red Cavalry and his eventual acceptance by the Cossack warriors. He is the perfect vehicle to mediate between the two halves of the book. Part of the Cossacks yet not a Cossack, Jew yet a stranger to the Jewish ghettoes of eastern Poland and the Ukraine, he allows his eye to roam freely over the passing scene. The *skaz* stories further distance him from the surrounding violence, for these frequently place accounts of awful brutality into the mouths of semiliterate characters very much unlike him. Lyutov is both soldier and tourist, insider and outsider, and through his dual role he brings a double focus to the book. As soldier he is the protagonist of a narrative that becomes the object of our interest; as tourist he takes us on a journey of discovery. He is the book's governing consciousness, filtering through his mind the unfamiliar roads of war and the exotic cultures of the wayside.[4]

Though the imagery associated with the action of war is often colorful, lush, even gorgeous, the syntax is terse, compact, ascetically simple. The prose is crafted into a complex counterpoint of ornamental magnificence of imagery and austere severity of style:

Fields of crimson poppy flower around us, a noon-time breeze plays in the yellowing rye, virginal buckwheat looms on the horizon like the wall of a distant monastery. The silent Volyn bends, the Volyn moves away from us into the pearly haze of birch groves, it crawls into the flowering hills and with loosening arms entangles itself in thickets of hops. An orange sun rolls along the sky like a lopped-off head, a tender light flares in the gorges of clouds, the standards of the sunset fly over our heads. The smell of yesterday's blood and of slaughtered horses drips into the evening chill. The blackened Zbruch roars and twists the foamy knots of its rapids. The bridges are down, and we ford the river. A majestic moon rests on the waves. The horses enter the water to their cruppers, the resounding torrents run through hundreds of horses' legs. Someone sinks and loudly curses the Mother of God. The river is strewn with black squares of wagons, it is full of clamor, whistles, and songs, thundering above the serpentine trails of the moon and the luminous hollows.[5]

While the imagery plunges us into a world of high drama, the phrasing indicates resolute action. The passage has an unfailing regularity of syntactical structure, as every clause opens with a subject followed by a verb, usually active. Subordination is virtually nonexistent – the concluding participial phrase is the only word group that even approximates a subordinate clause. As in a film sequence, a panoramic view of large-scale action develops from a string of discrete images, each given equal force.[6] The compactness of phrasing, the repetitive subject-verb order, the accumulation of active verbs in the present tense make for an assertive, emphatic style.[7] Babel habitually spoke of his language in military terms: of the "army of words, . . . in which all kinds of weapons come into play," of iron stabbing with the force of a period at the right place, of short stories that should have "the precision of a military communiqué," and prose that "must be written in the same firm, straightforward hand one uses for commands."[8] His epic manner is aggressively masculine.

The dynamism of the prose is heightened by images that animate the scene. Natural objects, in metaphorically assuming human qualities, become participants in the movements of men: "an orange sun rolls along the sky like a lopped-off head"; the Volyn "with loosening arms entangles itself in thickets of hops"; "the breeze plays"; "the blackened Zbruch roars." Nature and man blend into a single totality, as the sunset flies over the heads of the warriors like military standards, and the thundering clamor of men merges with the roaring of the river's torrents.[9]

Richly colored landscapes, brilliant midday suns, florid sunsets provide Babel's usual backdrop for epical action: "We were moving to meet the sunset. Its foaming rivers flowed along the embroidered napkins of peasants' fields. The stillness turned pink."[10] "It was after two of an expansive July day. A rainbow web of heat shimmered in the air. Beyond the hilltops glittered a holiday band of uniforms and horses' manes, braided with ribbons."[11] "They rode side by side, in identical jackets and gleaming silver-striped trousers, on tall chestnut horses. Raising a shout the troops moved after them, and pale steel flashed in the ichor of the autumnal sun."[12]

Proud military standards regularly accompany these resplendent marches: "The standards of the sunset fly over our heads."[13] "On gilt staffs, bearing velvet tassels, magnificent standards fluttered in fiery pillars of dust."[14] "We listened to the song in silence, then unfurled our standards, and to the sounds of the thundering march burst into Berestechko."[15]

The vivid colors that clothe the Cossacks and the vigorous style that catches their movements mark their separateness from humdrum life. Like the heroes of Homer and traditional epic, they are outsize men, without innerness or subjectivity, inhabitants of a heroic universe apart from common culture.[16] Formulaic epithets capture their heroic largeness: "I beheld the masterful indifference of a Tatar khan and recognized the horsemanship of the celebrated Kniga, the headstrong Pavlichenko, the captivating Savitsky."[17] They stand aloof of ordinary human misery: "To the soothing accompaniment of the peasants' incoherent and desperate clamor, Zh. sought out that gentle pulsing in the brain which portends clarity and energy of thought. Feeling at length the right beat, he snatched the last peasant tear drop, snarled imperiously, and walked off to Headquarters."[18] Unsullied by the squalid and ravaged towns they pass through, indifferent to the suffering of their victims, the heroes reflect in their personal appearance the rarefied atmosphere of their enclosed field of force. The grays of day-to-day existence do not touch them. Savitsky, a paragon of masculine beauty, is shown in colors like those of the gaudy sky; the recurrent image of a standard, proudly phallic, evokes his heroic stature.

I wondered at the beauty of his giant's body. He rose, the purple of his riding breeches, the crimson of his tilted cap, the decorations on his chest cleaving the hut as a standard cleaves the sky. A smell of scent and the cloyingly sweet freshness of soap emanated from him. His long legs were like young girls sheathed to the neck in gleaming boots.[19]

The passage exemplifies the difficulty modern writers have in sustaining the epic note. The youthful narrator's admiration is sincere, and his awed sincerity just saves the portrait from travesty.[20] If we feel something a bit precious and self-conscious about this giant bathed in cloying perfumes, another splendid Cossack comes across as slightly theatrical: "He skillfully swung his well-proportioned athlete's body out of the saddle. Straightening his splendid legs, . . . magnificent and agile, he moved toward the expiring animal, as if he were on stage. Dolefully, it fixed its stubborn, deep eyes on Dyakov and licked some imperceptible command from his ruddy palm. Immediately the exhausted horse felt a dextrous strength flowing from this gray-haired, vigorous, and dashing Romeo."[21] Babel's Cossacks, though they demand our respect, are not spared his irony. The ironic touches, according to Viktor Shklovsky, were a way to make his hyperbolical heroes palatable to modern readers.[22]

The central opposition of *Red Cavalry*, formally that of epic and pathos, has received various thematic interpretations: the way of violence versus the way of peace, Cossack versus Jew, the new revolutionary order versus traditional society, noble savage versus civilized man, and a pair that may subsume all of these – nature versus culture.[23] Though criticism cannot manage without such formulae, they ought not blind us to the complexities and ambiguities of a text. Not all the Cossacks are beautiful, and few, if any, are noble. Many are "solitary, poor, nasty, brutish," sprung from a Hobbesian rather than Rousseauian nature. Nor are all the Jews men of peace; some, the narrator among them, choose the way of war. What is beautiful to Babel is the realm of heroic action. Individual Cossacks may be treated ironically, even comically. The heroic march itself is never mocked. It is always solemn.

Movement defines the epic mode. Adding history to the list of interpretive terms does not discredit previous readings but makes them more precise and adequate. Nature is necessity, what is given and not made, the weather we live in rather than the forms we create. Natural things exhibit motion; humans are capable of action-motions that result from conscious, purposive choice. As such, history in *Red Cavalry* is presented as a kind of natural occurrence. From the opening passage, where physical nature and human activity merge in a single awesome march, the work communicates a sense of portentous events. Armies are on the move, "striking the hammer of history upon the anvil of future ages," in the grandiloquent rhetoric of a Cossack officer.[24] But all this movement has a formless character. It is sheer motion rather than deliberate action, an elemental "Cossack flood,"[25] whose usual expression is random and terrible violence.[26] The future is being forged by the hammer of history, but for men like Lyutov, compelled to act in the present, that future is obscure. On the other hand, the Cossacks, who are shaping history, seem oddly indifferent to its outcome. For them the appeal of revo-lution is the opportunity it gives for free exercise of their powers, which they manifest in indiscriminate violence and mindless cycles of vengeance. As in Tolstoy's *War and Peace*, history is being made by men who have no idea of what it is they are making. The eyes of the heroes of *Red Cavalry* are riveted to the immediate present, the act of the moment, the event as pure event. When the aged Hasidic Jew, Gedali, protests the revolution in the name of the Messianic "sweet revolution" of joy and deliverance, the narrator, speaking in the name of the actual historical revolution, answers in a tautology: "[The revolution] cannot help shooting . . . because it is the Revolu-tion."[27] The revolution is what it is – a brute fact as ineluctable as the givens of the natural world. It will have momentous issue, but the focus of its participants, like the prose of the narrator, is on the concrete givens of immediate experience.

Brilliant and rhapsodic, the epic universe is also threatened with emptiness: "The brilliant sky loomed inexpressibly empty, as it al-ways is in time of danger."[28] Besides the regal standard, another recurring image for war is the desert or wasteland (pustynia):

"Afonka . . . dragged himself to his squadron, utterly alone, in the dusty blazing desert of fields."[29] "Beyond the window horses neighed and Cossacks shouted. The desert of war yawned beyond the window."[30] In the desert of war, men suffer "an eternal homelessness."[31] Some turn into beasts. Matvei Pavlichenko has a "jackal's conscience" and was "suckled by a she-wolf";[32] Afonka Bida roams the countryside slaughtering Poles like a "lonely wolf."[33] When life is reduced to pure motion, empty of purpose, deprived of the nurture and restraints of culture, men turn into wild animals, or they feel themselves "utterly alone." The man without a city, Aristotle tells us, becomes either a beast or a god.[34] What escapes him is the specifically human. The epic line of unceasing motion ultimately resolves in exhaustion. Apparently the burden of being other than human is hard.

> We made the crossing from Khotin to Berestechko. The troops were dozing in their tall saddles. A song gurgled like a stream running dry. Monstrous corpses lay upon the ancient burial mounds. . . . Divisional Commander Pavlichenko's felt cloak fluttered over the staff like a gloomy flag.[35]

> *I've clearly understood how unfit I am for the work of destruction,*
> *how difficult it will be for me to free myself from my old ways – from*
> *that which is perhaps bad, but which smells like poetry to me, as the*
> *beehives smell of honey. . . . Some are going to cause revolution, and I*
> *am going to sing of that which is off to the side, which lies deeper.*
> *Isaak Babel (13 August 1920)*[36]

"Pathos" is Greek for suffering, and "passive" is from the Latin *passivus* or capable of suffering. To suffer is to endure or bear, to be passive, not to act. In moving from the epic mode to the pathetic, *Red Cavalry* turns from action to passivity. The worlds of culture exist in stasis. The prose loses its dynamism, as it departs from renderings of movements to portraits of conditions. Ruined Gothic churches and deserted castles epitomize Poland in Babel's book:

The breath of an invisible order flickered under the ruins of the priest's house, and its insinuating seductions unmanned me. O crucifixes, tiny as the talismans of courtesans, parchment of Papal Bulls and satin of women's letters, rotting in the blue silk of waistcoats! . . . I see the wounds of your god, oozing seed, a fragrant poison intoxicating virgins. . . . Beyond the window the garden path shimmered beneath the black passion of the sky. Thirsty roses swayed in the darkness. Flashes of green lightning flamed amid the cupolas. A naked corpse sprawled along the slope. The moonlight streamed over lifeless legs thrust apart. Here is Poland, here is the proud sorrow of the *Res Publica*!37

The intransitive verbs, most of them reflexive (*mertsalo, perelivaet-sia kolyshutsia, pylaiut, valiaetsia, struitsia*), describe motions that remain frozen in place. Where the verbs depicting the epic march of the army emphasize discrete events in time – "a tender light flares," "we ford the river," "the horses enter the water" – these convey states of objects rather than events or acts. The length of the verbs, their open syllables, the profusion of liquids (not limited to the verbs) slow the tempo of the prose and contribute to its "insinuating" quality. Interspersed into the passage are verbless exclamations ("crucifixes") that show the passage for what it is, a static evocation of a world: "Here is Poland . . . !"

This languid style and hothouse imagery of putrefaction and silky perversity are in the manner of fin de siècle decadence. In leaving the brilliant sunlight of war, we enter a Poland mirrored in Gothic moonlight. A sinister green hue and watery shades replace the regal purple and bright red, orange, and yellow of the heroic landscape: "The moon, green as a lizard, rose above the pond. From my window I could make out the estate of the Counts Raciborski – meadows and hopfields, hidden by the watery ribbons of twilight."38

Jewish places are depicted through catalogues of objects – a stasis of dead things.

Here before me is the market and the death of the market. The fat soul of plenty is dead. Dumb padlocks hang upon the booths, and the granite pavement is as clean as the bald pate of a corpse. There were buttons and a dead butterfly. . . . [Gedali] wound in and out of a labyrinth of globes, skulls, and dead flowers, waving a many colored feather duster of cock's plumes and blowing dust from the dead flowers. . . . A vague odor of corruption enfolded me.[39]

A brief evocation of a Jewish cemetery entitled "The Cemetery at Kozin" provides a metaphor for this dead world. It is almost verbless: of its four verbs, two are the statives "stand" and "lie"; a third is "sing," as the inscriptions on the stones sing to us of men and a way of life that is now only a memory.

> "Azrael son of Ananias, lips of Jehovah.
> Elijah son of Azrael, a mind waging lonely battle with oblivion.
> Wolff son of Elijah, prince robbed from the Torah in his nineteenth spring.
> Judah son of Wolff, Rabbi of Krakow and Prague. O death, O covetous one, O greedy thief. why couldst thou not have spared us, just for once?"[40]

Jewish scenes are evoked in this incantatory, quasi-liturgical style or, at other times, in a starkly naturalistic manner. Excrement is a recurring detail. Where the heroic world is expansive and sunlit, the Jewish is cramped and sunless: "At the back of the house there stretches out a shed of two, sometimes three stories. The sun never penetrates here. . . . In wartime the inhabitants seek refuge from bullets and pillage in these catacombs. Human offal and cow dung accumulate here for days. Depression and horror fill the catacombs with the corrosive and foul acidity of excrement."[41] Babel often portrays the Jewish Pale, as he does Catholic Poland, in the shadows of evening, but instead of the moon, a lonely star, the harbinger of the Jewish Sabbath, follows Lyutov on his nighttime wanderings.

The counterpoise of Cossack vigor and Polish-Jewish decay seems to call for an obvious reading. The vital new order is hammering out the future on the battlefields of Eastern Europe; set against it is the "rot of old times" (*gnil' stariny*) – the outdated societies, transfixed in immobility, that "reek while waiting for the new era."[42] The great watershed of the Russian Revolution made comparisons of the old and the new an obsessive preoccupation of early Soviet literature. But for complex minds like Babel's, the schemata into which we place life are starting points and not the culmination of artistic exploration. If the epic line of the book – the movement of war and history – is vibrant and compelling, it is also barren – a desert of the heart. The old ways are in decay, but it is among them that Lyutov seeks physical and spiritual nourishment. True, he occasionally finds sustenance in the form of comradeship among the Cossacks. The Cossacks are men too, and they must also take time from the incessant motion of war to look for relief in the ordinary habits of life. One of the important discoveries in Lyutov's education is that the Cossacks, for all their anarchic violence, have codes of honor by which they live.

But it is usually to the wayside – to old Poland and especially the Jews – that Lyutov turns for nourishment to sustain him in the desert. The taking of food is a central image of the book – one that acquires sacramental value. Evenings Lyutov drinks "the wine of [the artist Pan Apolek's] conversation";[43] he delights in "the food of the Jesuits," though it is strange, even ominous: "These cakes . . . had an odor of crucifixes. A cunning juice was in them, together with the aromatic fierceness of the Vatican."[44] To his fellow Jews he turns for more homely fare: "Gedali, . . . today is Friday, and it's already evening. Where are Jewish biscuits to be got, and a Jewish glass of tea, and a bit of that pensioned-off God in a glass of tea?"[45]

The discovery of nourishment in places marked by rot and excrement marks the enigmatic and paradoxical quality of culture in *Red Cavalry*. Culture lies on the wayside, tangential to the highway of revolution and war. Although the highway is straight and narrow and the men who pursue it single-minded, culture for Babel is a mysterious thing. It belongs to night, the moon, and the lonely Sabbath star rather than the clear sunlight of clamorous events. Its habitats are strange Gothic churches that emanate "the breath of invisible orders," lonely aristocratic gardens where statuary of "nymphs with gouged-out eyes lead a choral dance" under the green lizard of the moon, morgue-like rooms in which motley Jews, "the possessed, liars, and idlers" await the Messiah.[46] Out in the night lie temptations – of art, of prophetic vision, of nostalgia – that would lure Lyutov from the business of history. The "insinuating seductions" of the church at Novograd threaten to "unman" him. The Sabbath star draws him to memories of home and the enchantment of Jewish tradition: "On Sabbath eves I am wearied by the dense melancholy of memories. . . . Once on these evenings my child's heart rocked like a ship upon enchanted waves. O the rotted Talmuds of my childhood! I roam Zhitomir in search of a timid star."[47] Drawn to these mysteries, he consistently repels them to return to the incandescent world of activity: "Away, . . . away from these winking Madonnas."[48] "I took leave of Gedali and made my way back to the station. At the station, in the propaganda train of the First Cavalry Army, there awaited me the flare of hundreds of lights, the magical brilliance of the wireless station, the stubborn rush of the printing presses."[49]

The shift from the clear sunlight and martial rhythms of the epic to the mysterious moonlit nights and evocative language of the pathetic mode marks a change in kinds of experience. Language and imagery combine to determine the book's shape of feeling. In the daylight of the epic-heroic world, in the arena of history, which is man's inescapable circumstance, action is precise, unreflective, and violent. Life admits of clear-cut categorization, as humanity divides into agent and patient, actor and sufferer, forger of the future and remnant of the dying past. In the shadowy realm of human culture, where man gives himself to creation and thought instead of elemental motion, everything is hopelessly ambiguous: "I went along with [the moon], nursing unrealizable dreams and discordant songs."[50] Here Jews wallowing in excrement proffer nourishment; the dead and blind (Gedali is blind) are possessed by visions of eternal life; decadent landscapes tempt the narrator by the beauty and power of art.

Suffering itself – the pathos that defines the wayside, particularly the life of the Jews – resists a singleness of response. The Jews are shown as wretched and impotent, grotesque figures huddled in

squalid rooms, stinking of filth. But as they edge toward becoming
contemptible, they suddenly surprise us with their dignity. The first
story, "Crossing into Poland," can serve as a paradigm of the work's
contrast of Jew and Cossack. After the glorious opening march, we
are introduced into a hovel with "scraps of women's fur coats on the
floor, human feces, fragments of occult crockery." Jews "skip about
noiselessly, like monkeys, like Japs in a circus, their necks swaying
and twisting." And just when the contrast seems clear and tidy –
heroic beauty and grandeur versus the ugliness of suffering – one of
the pathetic victims bursts into a rhetoric of heroic stature that rivals
the heroism of the Cossack warriors: " 'Sir,' said the Jewess, . . . 'The
Poles cut his throat, and he begging them: Kill me in the backyard so
that my daughter won't see me die. But they did as suited them. He
died in this room, thinking of me. And now I'd like to know,' the
woman cried out with sudden and terrible power, 'I'd like to know
where in the world you could find another father like my father?' "[51]
Competing with the Cossack power of action is "the terrible power"
of Jewish and human suffering, "a power . . . of sorrow full of somber greatness."[52]

The representative figures of culture in *Red Cavalry*, the aged
Hasid Gedali and the Polish artist Pan Apolek, embody its mystery.
Jewish prophet and Polish artist and their societies – the Jewish Pale
and Catholic, aristocratic Poland – seem to denote for Babel the
ethical and aesthetic imaginations, respectively. Both Gedali and Pan
Apolek are incongruous and paradoxical figures, slightly comic, yet
visionary. "Old Gedali, the diminutive proprietor in smoked glasses
and a green frock coat down to the ground, meandered around his
treasures in the roseate void of the evening. He rubbed his small
white hands, plucked at his little gray beard, and listened, head bent,
to the mysterious voices wafting down to him."[53] Like Gedali, Pan
Apolek is a child of evening: "On fragrant evenings the shades of old
feudal Poland assembled, the mad *(iurodivyi)* artist at their head."
The description of this artist, whose "wise and beautiful life" goes to
Lyutov's head "like an old wine," is a study in incongruity: "In his
right hand Apolek carried a paintbox, and with his left he guided the

blind accordian player. The singing of their nailed German boots rang out with peace and hope. From Apolek's thin neck dangled a canary-yellow scarf. Three little chocolate-colored feathers fluttered on the blind man's Tyrolean hat. . . . it all looked as though . . . the Muses had settled . . . side by side in bright, wadded scarves and hobnailed German boots."[54]

Incongruous in appearance, Pan Apolek leads a life and pursues an art that are exercises in paradox. He is at one and the same time a decorator of Christian churches and a heretic. His favorite story is the apocryphal tale of Jesus lying with the virgin Deborah out of pity. In the presence of his art "a portent of mystery" touches Lyutov, and the mystery is of the ways the ordinary and mundane can become transfigured by art. Pan Apolek spends his life raising the poor and sinful to the condition of saints in icons of glorious color. "He has made saints of you in your lifetime," the indignant church authorities chide.[55] His artist's vision is but another version of the Hasid Gedali's prophetic dream of the coming Revolution of Joy and the International of Good People, of a community where there are no orphans in the house and every soul is given "first-category rations."[56] Polish village artist and Jewish shopkeeper, engulfed by brutality and violence, turn to dreams of universal compassion.

As action is the measure of man in the heroic-epic world of history, compassion is a cardinal value of culture. It provides the nourishment missing from the deserts of war. Night, which shrouds the landscapes of culture, is also a time of comfort. Whereas the images of day are masculine phallic standards cleaving brilliant sunlit skies, those of night are maternal: "Blue roads flowed past me like streams of milk spurting from many breasts";[57] "evening wrapped me in the life-giving moisture of its twilight sheets, evening laid a mother's hand upon my burning forehead";[58] "night comforted us in our sorrows, a light wind wafted over us like a mother's skirt."[59]

To the oppositions of *Red Cavalry* – epic and pathos, nature and culture, history and culture – we must add yet another: a masculine and a feminine-maternal attitude. The latter is specifically associated with Jewish values. Wrapped in "the dying evening," Gedali raises the image of the compassionate mother to a metaphysical principle.

All is mortal. Only the mother is destined for eternal life. And when the mother is no longer among the living, she leaves a memory which no one has yet dared to defile. The memory of the mother nourishes in us a compassion that is like the ocean. The measureless ocean nourishes the rivers that dissect the universe. . . . In the passionate edifice of Hasidism the windows and doors have been knocked out, but it is immortal, like the soul of the mother. With oozing eye sockets Hasidism still stands at the crossroads of the winds of history.[60]

And at the crossroads of the book stands the narrator-protagonist Lyutov, pulled one way by the claims of history and masculine action, the other by the allure of art and demands of compassion. Isaak Babel's great book continually circles a tragic dilemma. The cultures – artistic, religious, and moral – which nurture human life are dying. The march of history leaves men famished for spiritual nourishment; yet its imperatives will not be denied or evaded. The two realms – history and culture – are never brought into harmony, but the final two stories ("The Rabbi's Son" and "Argamak") seek out a middle ground.

We met the rebellious rabbi's son in an earlier story ("The Rabbi"), where he was presented as "the cursed son, the last son, the recalcitrant son."[61] By the end of *Red Cavalry* this last son of the rabbi's line has joined the Red Army, taken command of a regiment, and been mortally wounded. Like Gedali and Pan Apolek, Ilya is an ambiguous figure. His description points to features both male and female: "a youth . . . with the powerful brow of Spinoza, with the sickly face of a nun."[62] Lyutov, while going through the dying Ilya's belongings, discovers that he has lugged off to war emblems of all the opposites of the book: action and poetry, politics and art, things masculine and feminine.

Everything was strewn about pell-mell – mandates of the propagandist and notes of the Jewish poet. The portraits of Lenin and

Maimonides lay side by side, the knotted iron of Lenin's skull beside the dull silk of the portraits of Maimonides. A lock of woman's hair had been slipped into a volume of Resolutions of the Sixth Party Congress, and curved lines of Hebrew verse crowded the margins of Communist leaflets. They fell on me in a sparse and mournful rain – pages of the Song of Songs and revolver cartridges.[63]

This juncture of the opposing images suggests that Ilya has achieved a way not to reconcile the contradictions, but to live with them. Going off to war, he takes the baggage of culture with him. The tokens of culture lie side by side with those of war and history. The two poles remain, as they have been throughout the work, discrete antinomies. A mood of elegiac melancholy sweeps over Lyutov, as he once again stands face to face with the tragic incongruity of human life.

The mood is not one in which he or the rabbi's son will permit themselves to linger. Explaining to Lyutov why he went to war, Ilya says that, though formerly he would not abandon his mother, in a revolution a mother is only "an episode."[64] It is a pregnant remark, one that pertains at least as much to Lyutov's struggle as to Ilya's. We have seen that the opposition between action and culture also reflected the contraries of a masculine and feminine principle. On a psychological plane, the plot of Red Cavalry, its overarching action, is the story of Lyutov's liberation from the maternal image – from the passive, suffering side of his nature. Evening lays "a mother's hand" upon his "burning forehead," but it also crowns him with the thorns of martyrdom. His longing for the nourishing mother inhibits him from acting in the world of men. The terrible irony is that in order to enter that world in the context of war and revolution one must learn to kill: "Evening flew to the sky like a flock of birds, and darkness crowned me with its wet wreath. . . . Bent beneath a funereal crown, I moved on, imploring fate to grant me the simplest of capacities – the ability to kill my fellow man."[65] Over the course of the book Lyutov struggles against the webs of nostalgia that tie him to the mother, and in the final story ("Argamak") he breaks away to join the epic march of the Cossack army. He passes the test of mastering a horse – the sine qua non of Cossack manliness – and the Cossacks accept him: "I realized my dream. The Cossacks stopped watching me and my horse."[66] Committing himself to the realm of action, he finds his manhood.[67]

The maternal image and related images of nurture have been associated with culture and value. The mother, as progenitor of life and the center of the family, represents the continuity culture demands. In *Red Cavalry*, however, culture is also "episodic." The structures in which men and women live – family, nation, religion, art, tradition – appear to have a permanence that turns out to be illusory before the juggernaut of history. The dominant rhythm of *Red Cavalry* – the irrevocable epic march of revolution that is sweeping traditional culture into the dustbins of history – wins out. No wonder some critics have read the book as a renunciation of the values of culture and a celebration of primitivism.[68]

It is a mistaken reading. Culture is ultimately not an institution but an idea. As its institutions crumble in revolution, its idea is kept alive. For Gedali, the mother, even when dead, "leaves a memory," which is "immortal." It is surely no accident that the two most visible embodiments of culture in *Red Cavalry*, Gedali and Pan Apolek, are marginal men – Jewish mystic and Catholic heretic. Less tied than others to temporal institutions and orthodoxies, Gedali is able to feel confidence that his values, if not yet realized as actualities, will survive as memories to stand at the "crossroads of history."

At the end of the book the rabbi's son joins them to become the third and most important of the work's bearers of culture. As Apolek offered a model of the artist to Lyutov – "I vowed . . . to follow the example of Pan Apolek"[69] – the rabbi's son gives him a model for action. Lyutov feels a kinship with him stronger than any he knew before: "And I – scarcely containing the tempests of my imagination in my ancient body – I received the last breath of my brother."[70] *Brother* is not a word he could have conceivably used for any of the Cossacks, perhaps not even for Gedali and Pan Apolek. He joins the

Cossacks but he is too much a man of culture to go completely native. Gedali and Pan Apolek attract him by their commitment to values, both ethical and aesthetic, but they are dreamers and visionaries, too remote from the realities of history to teach him how to live in the world. The rabbi's son shows him a middle course. While participating actively in the violence, which he deems necessary, he keeps alive reminders of other ways: poetry, the thought of Maimonides, a lock of woman's hair. Choosing masculine action, he refuses to deny the feminine part of his nature. His decision is to live with the contradictions of culture and force.

These contradictions have engendered the controlling images of the book. They have become part of Lyutov's experience. In riding off with the Cossack army he of necessity takes them along. We have read *Red Cavalry* through the filter of his consciousness, so that they have become our experience as well. What he and we have experienced is the tragic character of human life. The resolution of *Red Cavalry* does not lie in the triumph of any particular allegiance or in synthetic reconciliation, but in an assertion of the will to act and live in a discordant world.[71]

NOTES

1. Renato Poggioli, "Isaak Babel in Retrospect," *The Phoenix and the Spider* (Cambridge, Mass.: Harvard University Press, 1957), p. 235. Unless noted otherwise, citations in this article are from I. E. Babel', *Konarmiia. Odesskie rasskazy, p'esy* (Letchworth: Bradda Books, 1965). Though based on a 1957 Soviet edition from which excisions have been made (for example, Trotskii's name has been deleted), it is the most readily available Russian version (hereafter cited as *Konarmiia 1965*). I have also consulted the first full Russian edition (excluding "Argamak," which Babel added in 1931), *Konarmiia* (Moscow-Leningrad: Gos. izd., 1926) (hereafter cited as *Konarmiia 1926*). Translations are largely my own, though I have borrowed from Walter Morison's able renderings (see Isaac Babel, *The Collected Stories*, translated by Walter Morison [New York: New American Library, 1960]). A literal translation of the title would be the more neutral "Horse Army," but I have stuck with the standard English title.

2. Babel is less interested in the region's Ukrainian peasantry, depicted in the book as an undifferentiated mass. In the civil war of 1918–20 between the Reds and Whites, the Cossacks largely sided with the latter, but the Polish campaign of 1920, which is the occasion of the book, witnessed a nationalistic reversal in reaction to the Polish intervention.

3. There is no mention of the Cossacks' notorious anti-Semitism in *Red Cavalry*, undoubtedly out of fear of censorship, but it is evident in the diary Babel kept in 1920, when he was serving as a journalist with the First Cavalry Army. He concealed his Jewish identity under the name Kirill Vasil'evich Liutov. Excerpts are quoted in the notes to other excerpts from his "Plans and Outlines for *Red Cavalry*" in *Literaturnoe nasledstvo*, 74 (1965): 490–99. A more extensive selection has been made in the United States, where editors do not have to shun unflattering facts of Soviet history or references to Jewish life (see Isaac Babel, *The Forgotten Prose*, edited and translated by Nicholas Stroud [Ann Arbor: Ardis, 1978], pp. 120–43).

4. "Babel saw Russia," writes Viktor Shklovskii, "as a French writer attached to Napoleon's army might have seen her" (Shklovskii, "I. Babel': Kriticheskii romans," *LEF*, no. 2 [1924], p. 154).

5. Babel, *Konarmiia 1965*, p. 23.

6. Eisenstein thought Babel could teach filmmakers "the specific texture of image and word and the technique of . . . the extreme laconicism of literature's expressive means" (Sergei Eisenstein, *Film Form: Essays in Film Theory* and *The Film Sense*, edited and translated by Jay Leyda [New York: Harcourt, Brace, 1957], p. 93).

7. Albert Cook speaks of "the simple declarative base" of epic and of "the relation between statement and rhythm [that] is one of contrast or counterpoint" (Cook, *The Classic Line: A Study in Epic Poetry* [Bloomington: Indiana University Press, 1966], p. 11).

8. Babel', "Guy de Maupassant," *Konarmiia 1965*, p. 262; Konstantin Paustovsky, "Reminiscences of Babel," in Patricia Blake and Max Hayward, eds., *Dissonant Voices in Soviet Literature* (New York: Pantheon, 1964), pp. 34–35.

9. Except for its modern tautness, Babel's prose recalls the lush and metaphoric prose of Russian romanticism, especially of Gogol' in works like "Taras Bulba."

10. Babel', *Konarmiia 1965*, p. 57.

11. Ibid., p. 98.

12. Ibid., p. 135.

13. Ibid., p. 23.

14. Ibid., p. 98.

15. Ibid., p. 87.

16. See Hermann Fränkel, "Der Homerische Mensch," in *Dichtung und Philosophie des frühen Grichentums*, 3d ed. (Munich: C. H. Beck, 1969), pp. 83–94. See also James M. Redfield's brilliant *Nature and Culture in the Iliad* (Chicago: 1975). Redfield writes: "The warrior stands on the frontier between culture and nature" *(Nature and Culture*, p. 101).

17. Babel', *Konarmiia 1965.* p. 66.

18. Ibid., p. 33.

19. Ibid., p. 49.

20. For another view, see Victor Terras, "Line and Color: The Structure of I. Babel's Short Stories in Red Cavalry," *Studies in Short Fiction* 3 (Winter 1966): 141–56.

21. Babel', *Konarmiia 1965*, p. 34.

22. "Clever Babel' is able to justify the beauty of his things by means of irony. Without it, it would be embarrassing to read him. He anticipates our objection and places a heading over his portraits – opera" (Shklovskii, "I. Babel': Kriticheskii romans," p. 154).

23. See Lionel Trilling's pioneering and brilliant introduction to the *Collected Stories*. The opposition of nature and culture is stated by Stanley Edgar Hyman, "Identities of Isaac Babel," *Hudson Review*, 8 (Winter 1956): 620–27. That Babel had in mind a contrast of culture and the Cossacks is suggested by a diary entry of 21 July 1920: "How I inhale the fragrance of Europe here [Poland]. And what about the Cossack? Traits: tale-bearing, professionalism, revolutionary spirit, bestial cruelty" (Babel, *Forgotten Prose*, p. 128).

24. Babel', *Konarmiia 1965*, p. 107.

25. Ibid., p. 39.

26. Babel's diary entry of 11 August 1920 includes the remark: "Heroic epopee. That is not a Marxist revolution, but rather a Cossack rebellion" (Babel', *Forgotten Prose*, p. 138).

27. Babel', *Konarmiia 1965*, p. 47.

28. Ibid., p. 99.

29. Ibid., p. 100.

30. Ibid., p. 55.

31. Ibid., p. 103.

32. Ibid., p. 76.

33. Ibid., p. 101.

34. Aristotle, *Politics* I.2.1253ª.

35. Babel', *Konarmiia 1965*, p. 87.

36. From an incomplete letter written at the front, addressee not given (Babel', *Forgotten Prose*, p. 139).

37. Babel', *Konarmiia 1965*, pp. 25–26.

38. Ibid., p. 88.

39. Ibid., pp. 46–47.

40. Ibid., p. 77.

41. Ibid., p. 88.

42. Ibid.

43. Ibid., p. 39.

44. Ibid., p. 25.

45. Ibid., p. 48.

46. Ibid., pp. 88, 89, 53.

47. Babel', *Konarmiia 1926*, p. 35. The reference to the Talmud was apparently deemed subversive by Soviet watchdogs of culture, for it has been excised from the 1957 edition.

48. Babel', *Konarmiia 1965*, p. 27.

49. Ibid., p 55.

50. Ibid., p. 41.

51. Ibid., pp. 23–14.

52. Ibid., p. 60.

53. Ibid., p. 46.

54. Ibid., pp. 35–36.

55. Ibid., pp. 35–39.

56. Ibid., pp. 47–48.

57. Ibid., p. 42.

58. Ibid., p. 51.

59. Ibid., p. 95.

60. Ibid., p. 53. Martin Buber describes the "Mother" as one of several conceptions "of the divine soul imprisoned in the material world" that were adopted by the Cabbala from Gnosticism and thence made their way into Hasidism. She is a being "who must walk through all the sufferings of the world of things . . . mediating between primal good and primal evil" (Buber,

The Origin and Meaning of Hasidism, edited and translated by Maurice Friedman [New York: Horizon, 1960], p. 118).

61. Babel', *Konarmiia 1965*, p. 55.

62. Ibid., p. 54.

63. Ibid., p. 146.

64. Ibid.

65. Ibid., p. 104.

66. Ibid., p. 152.

67. In "Zamost'e" he dreams that he has been crucified: a woman proffers her breast "like a nurse proffering food"; then, seeing himself dead, he hears her intone, "Jesus, receive the soul of thy departed servant," and awakes as "the back of a horse cleaves the sky like a black crossbar" (ibid., p. 127). Besides the moral dilemma, we find the ingredients of an Oedipal crisis in this overattachment to the mother, inability to take aggressive action, and fear of (or desire for) martyrdom (castration). In "My First Goose," a key story, he attempts to resolve the crisis by the symbolic act of killing a goose, which wins the Cossacks' approval. But the act is tawdry, and he is consumed by shame.

68. See Steven Marcus, "The Stories of Isaac Babel," *Partisan Review* 22, no. 3 (Summer 1955): 400–11.

69. Babel', *Konarmiia 1965*, p. 33.

70. Ibid., p. 147.

71. Robert Maguire writes that Liutov "longs to find an allegiance that will pull together all these conflicting and incomplete identities; yet circumstances compel him to make constant acts of allegiance that he knows fall far short of perfection" (Maguire, *Red Virgin Soil: Soviet Literature in the 1920s* [Princeton, N.J.: Princeton University Press, 1968], pp. 328–29).

Line and Color: The Structure of I. Babel's Short Stories in *Red Cavalry*

VICTOR TERRAS

The stories of Babel's *Red Cavalry* have been discussed often, almost invariably as a whole rather than as individual masterpieces. With good reason, for they *are* a whole in more ways than one. The homogeneity of setting and thematics is enhanced by the presence of a constant "I," presumably Babel himself, and by cyclic elements such as recurrent characters, events, and places. Certain conflicts recur so persistently critics have thought that the whole of *Red Cavalry* can be seen as a study in contrast and paradox.[1] For instance, the *contrast* between Babel's "lyric joy"[2] and the horrors of war he describes; the *paradox* of a bespectacled Jewish intellectual and pacifist appearing not only as a chronicler of the exploits of Budyonny's Red Cossacks, but also as their friend and companion-at-arms. Certain recurring stylistic traits, such as the frequent use of *skaz* technique or the lyric pathos that is rekindled in almost every story, add to this impression of homogeneity.

I will not dwell on these unifying traits. They have been recognized and described exceedingly well by Poggioli, Struve, and, best of all, by Lionel Trilling. I will, on the contrary, try to put in relief those traits that belong to a given story as such, which establish it as an artistic creation in its own right, which make for its peculiar beauty, harmony, and completeness. Such inquiry is, I think, justified on two counts: first, the *Red Cavalry* stories originally appeared one by one, in several journals, each attracting on its own merits the attention of the public and critics alike; second, the heterogeneous, even discordant, features of these stories are just as important as are the common and the unifying. At least I believe so and will now try to demonstrate why.

If we use Emil Staiger's existential conception of the epic, dramatic, and lyric modes of poetic creation,[3] the main themes of the stories in *Red Cavalry* must, I think, be distributed among all three genres.

There is, first of all, the epic theme of the ride to a strange place where adventure, passion, or even death are waiting: the ride to a rendezvous with destiny. Naturally the theme appears in "travesty" so to say,[4] Parsifal disguised in the ungainly uniform of a soldier of the revolution, Amfortas wearing the rags of a poor Polish Jew. In the very first tale, "Crossing into Poland," the "I" rides through the intoxicating beauty of a Ukrainian summer night, arriving at the ancient Volhynian town of Novograd past midnight. The poor Jewish home where he is billeted is turned into a haunted place by the grotesque nightmares that plague him when he finally falls asleep. In the end it reveals its solemn mystery. The old man at whose side the intruder has slept is not asleep but dead, murdered by the Poles the day before. His daughter's story then shows the old man to have died the glorious death of a martyr. The ride has taken our young adventurer to a sacred place, as well as to one of horrors.

The ride to a fateful encounter is a feature of several other stories. Pavlichenko, the avenger, returns to the estate of Nikitinsky, his former landlord, to get even with the old man for the wrong he has done him years ago, when the now Red general was herding Nikitinsky's cattle. The bizarre antics of the crazed lady of the manor turn the house into a "castle of horrors." The descent to the vaults of the mansion, where Nikitinsky, trembling for his life, shows Pavlichenko all his treasures, enhances this impression. The murder of the old man, a passionate yet purposeful act, is a fitting finale.

"Prishchepa's Vengeance" is thematically close to Matthew Pavlichenko's story. A young Cossack rides home to recover the property stolen by his neighbors after the Whites killed his parents. It culminates in a nightmarish orgy of revenge, destruction, and despair.

In "The Story of a Horse," a tale in a somewhat lighter vein, Commander Khlebnikov rides a hundred versts in a stretch to the legendary Savitsky's haunt, to claim the white stallion he loves. This time it is the intruder who is defeated. Khlebnikov returns without his white horse, a broken man.

In "The Road to Brody," Babel gives the theme of the ride a lyric treatment. The nostalgic ride through the tall cornfields of the Ukraine, under "blazing, winged skies," stops short of the dented stones of the synagogues of the sacred city. It merges with the condemned Cossack's ride to Heaven in Afonka Bida's song. And the song itself joins the ride, "trailing like smoke."

Some other stories are focused not on the ride, but entirely on the adventure at the end of the ride. In "The Church at Novograd" and in "In St. Valentine's Church" the adventurer enters the "aromatically fierce," forbidden and fascinating world of a Catholic church; in "The Rabbi" it is the equally exotic world of a Hasidic synagogue; in "Gedali" it is the strange microcosm of an old curiosity shop.

Several stories are thematically close to the mode of the legend, featuring a saint or a hero. "Sandy the Christ" is a *vita sancti*[5] – in travesty, of course – both explicitly and symbolically. Sandy, the simpleminded syphilitic and singer of songs, *is* a saint. He feels it himself; the Cossacks who call him "the Christ" know it no less than their women, who seek solace and comfort from him. And is Sandy's stepfather not a carpenter, and Sandy his helper? That he surrenders his mother to his stepfather to get permission to hire out as a shepherd, that he sleeps with women, that he is a soldier like the other Cossacks is the "travesty" part of it.

Another *vita sancti* is the story of Pan Apolek, God's fool, drunkard, blasphemer, and artist of genius, who is in a way Babel's double. The solemn proem sets a tone that keeps ringing over the irony of the narrative and triumphs in the clausule:

The wise and beautiful life of Pan Apolek went to my head like an old wine. In Novograd-Volynsk, a town crumpled in a hurry by the war, amid twisted ruins, fate threw at my feet a gospel that had lain concealed from the world. Surrounded by the simplehearted radiance of nimbi, I then made a vow to follow Pan Apolek's example. And the sweetness of meditative spite, the bitter scorn for the curs and swine of mankind, the fire of taciturn and intoxicating revenge – all this I sacrificed to my new vow.

In the stories "The Rabbi" and "The Rabbi's Son," Elijah Bratslavsky, last scion of a proud dynasty, is saint, hero, and prince all in one. The last words we hear from him are these: "I got to Kovel . . . The kulaks opened the front to the enemy. I took command of a scratch regiment, but too late. . . . I hadn't enough artillery."

The gentle poet, with the body of a boy and the wan face of a nun, was also a born leader of men. But the travesty is present even here: we meet the prince not only in defeat and despair, but also in shame and degradation. Babel shows some other heroes in more conventional epic situations of the human condition: victory or heroic death in battle. "The Brigade Commander" is a bright picture of ambition, strength, and triumph. The bowlegged peasant boy Kolesnikov is awkward and nervous before Budyonny, but not so when he faces his brigade, much less the enemy. Budyonny, the Cossacks, and the narrator himself, all watch the young man's first, victorious command performance with obvious pleasure. This is a Homeric episode – in travesty, for Kolesnikov, a fine soldier who fights "for glory," as befits the true hero, who after his victory displays "the masterful indifference of a Tartar Khan," is externally a drab and even a ridiculous figure!

Another Homeric episode in travesty can be found in "Konkin's Prisoner." The cocky Red hero, thrice Knight of the Order of the Red Banner, tells without boasting, "in his customary farcical manner," how eight well-armed Polish horsemen are easy game for two battle-weary Cossacks, one of whom has been badly wounded earlier in the day. An elderly Polish general is cornered after putting up a brave fight. The old man's love of life gets the better of his honor and he is inclined to hand over his sword. Much as in similar Homeric scenes, the balance, after a good deal of suspense, tilts toward Hades: the general is done in by his captors after all.

"Chesniki" could have been called "Before the Battle," had not the following story been "After the Battle." We see at first Red cavalry getting ready for one of its headlong charges. The demigods Voroshilov and Budyonny are personally directing operations. Then, much as it would in the *Iliad*, the scene shifts to an idyllic microcosm. Sasha, the Red amazon, is secretly getting her mare covered by the commander's prize stallion. The beginning of the following story then brings one of the most stirring battle scenes in all Russian literature: the unforgettable cavalry charge of Chesniki.

In "Squadron Commander Trunov" the glory of a heroic death is only slightly dimmed by the usual travesty. The slaughter of the prisoners by the doomed Trunov acquires a mythic meaning if we perceive them as the sacrificial victims that accompany the epic hero in death. The very futility of Trunov's death has a certain grandeur about it. The American planes of Major Fauntleroy's air squadron, which kill swiftly, efficiently, and inexorably, are like intruders from another, superior world. Trunov challenges them, and dies like an epic hero who has challenged the gods. But the petty, squalid details of the setting disguise the main theme, enough for us to take the heroic epic poem for a naturalistic war sketch.

The elements of travesty are stronger in "The Widow," the story of the death of Commander Shevelyov. He dies, to his last breath a hero and a leader, against a background of revolting animal life. Who would recognize the rivalry for the arms of the slain Achilles in the squabble for the dead hero's earthly belongings? But if we take an unprejudiced look at the theme of this story, and at those of the other "epic" stories in *Red Cavalry*, we see that they are in fact the common themes of the heroic epos of all times. It is most important to note that this is not merely a self-evident concomitant of the fact that Babel is writing about war and that his heroes are soldiers. The point is that the *sujets* of these stories reflect a vision of the human condition that is characteristic of a heroic worldview, of a heroic society.[6]

A good many of the stories in *Red Cavalry* feature a dramatic rather than an epic theme, for example, a conflict based on social tensions. It is to this type of story that many of the interesting comments made about Babel do particularly apply. It is mostly in these dramatic stories that Babel's ironies and ambiguities are in evidence: dramatic pathos thrives on such tensions, not epic ethos.

The easiest recognized of these tensions is that between the intellectual, usually represented by Babel's "I," and the Cossack. It may develop along many different vectors: the natural pacifist clashing with the man for whom killing, nay murder, is a business; the abjectness of the thinking man faced with a situation that calls for outright, courageous action – such as putting a bullet through a dying soldier's head to save him from being abused by the approaching enemy; the battle between the subtle irony of "specs," the commissar, and the unsuspecting good humor and exuberant physical vigor of the Cossacks and their handsome giant of a commander, a battle that both parties win and lose: the bespectacled law school graduate cannot help becoming enamored of Savitsky's imposing physique and reckless élan; also, for all his outward bravado, he knows all too well that he will always remain but a sorry killer – even of geese; the Cossacks could not ever, like their commissar, spy out the secret curve of Lenin's line, they naively see only what the learned man wants them to see as he reads the leader's latest speech to them. And the semiliterate Savitsky, for all his manly charm, cuts a fairly ridiculous figure as a writer of military prose.

The most dramatic of all the stories in *Red Cavalry* is perhaps "Argamak." The world of *Red Cavalry* is a horseman's world in which the "I" must play the role of an intruder. In "Argamak" the intruder becomes doubly odious when given the Cossack Tikhomolov's mount Argamak. Also, although this is never made explicit, the man who is ruining Tikhomolov's glorious stallion is obviously a man of some authority, namely, a political commissar. The tensions developing from this situation are many: Tikhomolov, the disgraced Cossack, fights to recover the horse that must be as dear to him as his life. He finally succeeds, by a feat of extraordinary bravery. The "I" struggles to gain the friendship of the Cossacks – in vain. He also struggles to conquer Argamak, who hates his involuntary tormentor no less than does Tikhomolov. There is also a conflict, hidden and subtle, between "line" and "color." Baulin, the squadron leader, is a genuine Bolshevik: "The path of his life had been laid down, and he had no doubts as to the correctness of this path." Only the *line* matters to Baulin; passion, suffering, beauty are irrelevant. The pathetic story of Argamak is to him a routine disciplinary matter. The emotional, ethical, and aesthetical (yes, for is it not a crime against beauty to give a great horse to a miserable horseman?) angles do not exist for him; they nearly kill the sensitive Babel.

The conflict between "line" and "color," which erupts openly and with great acerbity in such later stories as the one that actually bears the title "Line and Color," or "Froim Grach," can be recognized in some *Red Cavalry* stories as well.[7] The story "Evening" shows it quite clearly. Galin, the walleyed communist fanatic, is absolutely confident of the victory of his party, whose line is likened to a pair of railroad tracks. It is Galin who utters the following prophetic words:

> You're a driveler, and we are fated to have to put up with you drivelers. We're busy shelling and getting at the kernel for you. Not long will pass and then you'll see that cleaned kernel, and take your fingers out of your nose and sing of the new life in no ordinary prose. In the meantime sit still, you driveler, and stop whimpering around us.[8]

Line will win over color. There is little consolation in the circumstance that Galin pays a price for his victory: he loses the contest for the graces of Irina, the laundress. Having sleepily listened to his tirades, she goes off to bed with Vasily, the cook.

Babel's dramatism depends on tensions between men, classes, nationalities, not on a man's inner conflicts. Dostoyevskian complexities or the isolation of the Chekhovian dramatic hero will not easily be found in *Red Cavalry*. Babel's drama is that of head-on clash. Hostility or loneliness, much rather than alienation or solipsism, trouble the Babelian hero.

Struve has pointed out, very shrewdly, I think, that there is something romantically conventional about most of Babel's characters.[9] They do what we expect them to do. Almost invariably we meet them in moments of high crisis and so only see the highlights of their roles, so to speak. In other words, the Babelian character is devised to dramatize one of the tensions inherent in the world of *Red Cavalry*. We are shown the tension, not the whole man.

It is in its dramatic capacity that the Babelian short story takes on some of the traits of social satire. Such is the case in "Salt," one of Babel's most famous stories, which dramatizes the unholy union between tough revolutionary phraseology and the self-righteous brutality of the semiliterate. Another such story is "A Letter," with the eternal theme of father and sons fighting on different sides. The element of travesty is particularly strong in the latter story, so strong it almost turns it into a satirical allegory. The tragic pathos of fratricidal civil war is dragged through the mud of the narrator's low mentality and dulled by the brutish callousness of the principals of the drama. The heroic combat of Hildebrand and Hadubrand is replaced by two sadistic executions.

Several of the stories not mentioned so far display a strong affinity to a modern genre which for want of a better term I shall call *the nightmare:* a piece the mode of perception and structure of which resemble an oppressive dream. "Italian Sunshine" is a good example. Its hero, Sidorov, obviously is an executioner of the Cheka who is on the verge of "cracking up" (or has he already crossed the threshold?). He dreams of being sent to Italy to organize the assassination of King Victor Emmanuel, but would, if worse came to worst, accept an assignment with the Odessa Cheka. The ravings of Sidorov, the "melancholy murderer," are set against the background of the "I's" own, almost somnambulant stream-of-consciousness.

"Zamoste" is another dreamlike piece, shreds from the stream-of-consciousness of a desperately tired man, alternating with dream scenes. The violent clashes in "After the Battle" are experienced as if in a trance: important details remain untold, the sequence of events is sharply discontinuous.

A few stories are rather easily recognized as "poems in prose," thus belonging to the lyric genre, for example, "The Cemetery at Kozin," "The Road to Brody," and "The Song." The lyric mode also prevails in "Gedali" and in "Berestechko." The remaining pieces can be classified as *feuilletons*. There are not too many of them: "Discourse on the Tachanka," "The Remount Officer," "The Story of a Horse, Continued," and "Treason."

We see, then, that although the setting and characters of *Red Cavalry* are quite uniform indeed, the structural-aesthetic thematics of these stores are extremely varied. The same Cossacks and Jews, soldiers and civilians, insensitive brutes and subtle dreamers appear in situations the aesthetic and emotive mode of which may be either epic or dramatic, heroic or satirical, sublime or comical, serious or frivolous. Such heterogeneity does not suggest per se that the stories of *Red Cavalry* do not follow the traditional canon of the classical novella. We know that it is in the structure rather than in the *sujet* that we find the distinctive traits of this well-defined genre. So let us ask: Do we find in Babel's stories the straight line of action, the limited but compact space, the dramatically coiled spring of time, all of which are characteristic of the novella from Boccaccio to Guy de Maupassant?[10]

I believe that the stories written entirely, or almost entirely, in *skaz* must be set aside as a separate structural type. Style is here the principal integrating factor. The author's determination to create a credible semblance of uneducated narrative is binding not only stylistically but also structurally. And do Kurdyukov's letter to his mother, Balmashev's letter to the editor of the *Red Trooper*, or the complaint of the three hospitalized Cossacks in "Treason" ramble along, mixing the relevant with the irrelevant, the serious with the comical, the touchingly sincere and poignantly true with the stupidly affected, brazenly phony rhetoric of the semiliterate.

The uneducated or semiliterate narrator finds it difficult to get to the point of his tale as he wades through a morass of irrelevant trivialities; when he finally does get there, it is awkwardly off balance, and as if by accident. The murders in "Salt" and in "A Letter" seem just to happen, anticlimactically almost; and in "Treason" we discover, late in the story and among other things, that one of the three principals died four days after the incident described by his buddy. The entire narrative in these stories is characterized by what one might call "wrong accents" – stylistically, structurally, and emotionally.

Although the stylized stories are among the best remembered, they do not, I believe, represent Babel's art at its loftiest. I think that Babel's claim to immortality rests entirely with those stories that reveal the stream-of-consciousness of a cultured, sophisticated, aesthetically and emotionally sensitive young man – young even though there may be "autumn in his heart."

Clearly plot in the conventional sense (the Russian *fabula*) is not what gives unity to most of Babel's stories. In fact, the tales in which plot seems to play its customary role are mostly those written in *skaz* and, in my opinion, the least ambitious artistically. In many of the other stories we observe a curious phenomenon: what would have to be the plot of the story is condensed into a brief scene, or even into a single phrase, and made a distinct, concrete part of the narrative. Figuratively speaking, the plot is then a single figure on the face of a rug, not a pattern woven into the whole rug.

The martyr's death of the old Jew in "Crossing into Poland" is told in a few lines at the very end of the story. In "The Rabbi's Son" the story of Elijah's heroic stand and tragic failure appears as if in parentheses. In "The Rabbi" the fascinating image of the last prince of the dynasty remains in the background and the story of his rebellion, glory, and tragic end is only hinted at even though Elijah is the hero of that tale also.

In "The Church at Novograd" the story of Pan Romuald's treason and death flashes by in a subordinate clause. In "Italian Sunshine" the mad, sordid career of Sidorov, the ex-anarchist and now Chekist, emerges from the chaos of the second page of his letter; his roommate, who tells the story, dared not look for the beginning.

Some stories are veritable mosaics of intriguing, dynamic themes, each of which would be good for a fine short story. In the difficult-to-analyze story "Berestechko," for instance, introduced in order are an old Ukrainian with a bandore, singing of the ancient glory of the Cossacks; the murder of an old Jew, accused of spying; mad ninety-year-old Countess Raciborska, who would beat her son with a coach-man's whip because he had given the dying line no heir; and the echo of a story of love and separation in a French letter dated "Be-restechko, 1820."

Although Babel seems to be scornful of plot in the conventional sense, the clausule (Russian *kontsovka*) of the classical novella is very much in evidence throughout. However, much as with the plot, what looks like the "clausule" is sometimes a separate entity, independent of the rest of the story. It may come in the form of an elegant conclusion of the plot, as for instance in "Argamak," "Konkin's Pris-oner," or "Afonka Bida"; as a lyric recapitulation of the subjective, emotional mood of the story, as in "Gedali," "My First Goose," or "After the Battle"; as a rhetorical peroration, as in "The Rabbi's Son," "Berestechko," or "The Cemetery at Kozin"; or as a brief, poignant gnome, as in "The Church at Novograd," "Story of a Horse," or "The Life and Adventures of Matthew Pavlichenko."

In many instances we see a definite rondo pattern (Russian *kol'tso*); the clausule returns to the proem, as for instance in "Squadron Commander Trunov," "Evening," "Pan Apolek," or "Gedali."

Clearly there could not be any greater variety. The same can be said of the exposition. A terse, matter-of-fact statement in the style of a military communiqué is the usual introduction ("Our division took Berestechko last night"). But this is deceptive. What follows is more often than not a colorful image – a landscape, a portrait, or a *nature morte*. Besides, Babel has many other ways to start a story: with a rhetorical proem ("The Rabbi's Son," "Pan Apolek," "Eve-ning"), with a dialogue ("The Rabbi"), by taking the reader *in medias res* with a narrative passage ("The Death of Dolgushov"), or by raising the curtain with a description ("My First Goose").

Really nowhere – with the exception of the *skaz*-type stories – do we have anything resembling conventional epic narrative. There are but few dialogues of any length. What we have is a kaleidoscopic sequence of descriptions of town and country; Goyaesque[11] scenes of violence and suffering; brief, racy dialogues (always "stylized"!); stream-of-consciousness-type passages; dreams and nightmares; rhe-

torical passages ringing with emotion; gnomes and bons mots; anecdotes, biographies, legends compressed into a single paragraph;
scraps of "confessions"; a torrent of similes and metaphors which
often enough are motives in their own right. Here, for example, is a
breakdown into motives for "Crossing into Poland":

An introductory line in the tone of a military communiqué.[12]
Then, as early as in the second sentence, "color" joins "line" in the
form of first an adjective (the rearguard of the advancing army is
called "clamorous"), then an adjectival phrase which is a story all in
itself ("over the highroad from Brest to Warsaw built by Nicholas I
upon the bones of peasants") Half a page of elaborate landscape
painting follows. Toward the end of this description the movements
and noises of the army marching through the peaceful countryside
take over. The connecting phrase "far on in the night we reached
Novograd" opens up a very different picture, the *intérieur* of a poor
Jewish home, with its silent, puppetlike occupants.

At this point, the first line of dialogue is spoken: "Clean this up," I
said to the woman. "What a filthy way to live!" The Jews silently
clean up and make the unwanted visitor's bed: a brief, but oppressive,
nightmarish description.

After the connecting phrase "silence overcame all," another lyric
nature image (of the moon), and then another connecting phrase and
a vivid, dramatic, grotesque nightmare dreamed by the "I." It is
disrupted, finally, by the phrase "and here I woke up, for the pregnant woman was groping over my face with her fingers."

Here, then, comes the first significant dialogue line which, flash-
like, brings the woman to life: "Good sir," she said, "you're calling
out in your sleep and you're tossing to and fro. I'll make you a bed in
another corner, for you're pushing my father about." And now the
ghastly revelation, in curt, dispassionate words, that the intruder had
been pushing about a man whose throat "had been torn out and his
face cleft in two."

Finally, the Jewess tells the story of her father's death. The narrator inserts an observation on the intonation of her voice. The
woman's last words, which conclude the story, form a rhetorical

question, uttered "with sudden and terrible violence": "I want to know where on earth you could find another father like my father?" The story is quite typical of *Red Cavalry*. In longer stories we have, of course, even more different motives. The question arises: How are these many different motives, which are often quite heterogeneous in more than one respect, put together to form the marvelously integrated organism of the Babelian short story? This question is all the more legitimate as Babel himself is reported, by a reliable source, to have seen his creations as assemblages of motives, integrated by painstaking craftsmanship:

> When I write down the first version of a story, the manuscript looks disgusting, simply horrible! It's an aggregate of more or less successful bits, joined together by the dreariest connecting links, so called "bridges," a kind of dirty ropes. [. . .] This is where my work begins. I check sentence after sentence, and not once, but many times. First of all I throw out the superfluous words from each sentence. [. . .] And so I go on, retyping the text each time, until I get to the point where, despite the most savage captiousness, I couldn't find a speck of dirt in the manuscript.[13]

This gives us a valuable hint: we may view Babel's stories as compositions rather than as narrative prose in the conventional sense. As far as their genesis is concerned, they are closer to the lyric poem than to the epic narrative. A Babelian short story owes its completeness and unity to composition, more than to an inherent thematic or structural principle (such as plot, adherence to the established rules of a specific genre, or a dominating character).[14]

Some recurring structural devices of Babel's stories resemble lyric more than epic or dramatic technique. The importance as well as the various specific types of the clausule are traits the novella shares with the lyric poem, as is the rondo form found so often in Babel's stories. However, more often than not, the proem or the clausule or both are distinctly lyrical, particularly when they consist of an image or of a rhetorical ejaculation, which is often. It is also my impression that the frequent recurrence of a motive (usually an image) in the same story resembles a lyrical refrain as much as it does the "falcon" of the classical novella.[15] I am thinking here of such items as the blood trickling through the bandage wrapped around Trunov's head, the shepherd-saint motive in "Sandy the Christ," or the blinking of Galin's walleye.

Babel's is a static space, filled with vivid, sensuous images. Savitsky's gigantic frame cleaves the hut "as a standard cleaves the sky." Afonka Bida comes galloping "framed in the nimbus of the sunset." Kolesnikov walks to glory "bathed in the crimson haze of a sunset that seemed as unreal as oncoming death." A comparison of Babel's space with that in the paintings of the young Chagall has been rightly suggested.[16] The space of both artists is space without a boundary, none even between heaven and earth. In this continuum of color there float images – some beautiful, some sordid; some delicately ethereal, some coarsely naturalistic; images of the peasants and Jews of Red Russia, their little towns, their huts, their horses and their cattle; and the moon in the most incredible, yet so real shades of color.

For the poet, *color* is of course a somewhat broader concept than for the painter, although in Babel's case the literal (rather than metaphoric) meaning of that word applies often enough. *Color* is the enchanting moonlit night into which are cast "dreams leaping about like kittens," "a satin-clad Romeo singing of love," Sidorov's mad letter under a flickering candle, a squabbling Jewish couple, a melancholy murderer's dream of Italian sunshine. *Color* is the fiery sunset over peaceful Ukrainian cornfields in "Crossing into Poland," "The Death of Dolgushov," "The Brigade Commander," and "The Road to Brody." *Color* is the "burning brilliance of the skies" over "blue dust and Galician mournfulness" in the story "Squadron Commander Trunov." *Color* is the melancholy Sabbath eve atmosphere in "Gedali" and "The Rabbi."

The arrangement of images, shreds of dialogue, scraps of confession and stream-of-consciousness, rhetorical passages and aphorisms in this space of color likewise resembles the composition of Chagall's paintings. Time in *Red Cavalry* is not time as we know it from the classical novella or even from the Chekhovian short story. It may be the leisurely change of evening to night, or of night to morning. It may be the unnoticed flow of the "I's" stream-of-consciousness, often quite timeless like a dream. Never is it the sharply felt time of anticipation or regret. When there is action, time seems to be standing still. The cavalry charge of Chesniki is for us the static image of a "deathlike wall of black uniforms and pale faces" and Captain Yakovlev awaiting the charge with unsheathed saber, a gold tooth gleaming in his mouth, and his black beard lying on his chest "like an icon on a dead man."

Not that the Babelian short story has not got line. What it hasn't got is a line typical of it, as the curve is of the Chekhovian short story. In *Red Cavalry* a good deal seems to depend on the theme of each story. In the more "epic" stories the initial bold sweep of the line one sees in the opening paragraph of so many stories does not altogether dissolve into color, but continues, sometimes firm and clear, sometimes a mere hazy outline, straight to the climax of the story. Such are the stories featuring the epic ride to a rendezvous with destiny.

The stories of the life and death of a hero, or of a saint, tend to follow the rondo form. The substance of the "legend" is revealed in the solemn proem; the story itself then brings various vivid details, not necessarily in chronological order; and the conclusion is another encomium, echoing the mood, or even the image, of the proem. Such is the pattern of "Pan Apolek," "Squadron Commander Trunov," and "Sandy the Christ."

As to the dramatic tales, they all share the permanent unresolvedness of their conflicts. The tension between Cossack and bespectacled Commissar that is felt at the very beginning of "My First Goose" or "After the Battle" is only heightened by the several clashes that make up the plot of the story. The conclusion underscores, in each case, that the rift is irremediable. In this may lie the completeness of the story.

The ironies and ambiguities of Babel's art do not, I believe, create a "curve." The irony, if present, is constant and almost immediately obvious, as in the *skaz*-type stories, where the stylistic contrast between Babel's introductory words and the following *skaz* creates tension immediately.[17] Nor does the mask of Babelian travesty deceive us: we soon recognize heroes and saints, leaders and martyrs, good men and murderers, in spite of their disguises.

A few times an ambiguity does seem to make for a structural break. In "Gedali" one has the feeling that the narrator is presenting to us a historical relic, a glimpse of the vanishing past, for which reason has but little regret, in spite of heart's nostalgia – then suddenly this line: "She cannot do without shooting, Gedali, because she is the Revolution." This changes the mood of the story and introduces the ambiguity. With the brash young revolutionary having nothing better to offer to refute Gedali's simple philosophy, the old man's naiveté becomes wisdom.

In "The Rabbi" the atmosphere suddenly changes when, among the possessed, the liars, and the idlers, we perceive suddenly "a youth with the face of Spinoza, with Spinoza's powerful brow and the wan face of a nun." A little later the Rabbi chants: "Blessed is the Lord God of Israel Who hath chosen us from amongst all the nations of the earth." This would have been pure irony with Cossack horses neighing under the windows of the synagogue but for the presence of the chosen youth, the prince. In "The Rabbi's Son" the break comes when we hear, to our intense gratification, that Elijah had proven himself a prince not only in spirit but in action as well. Yet this kind of structural break effected through the introduction of an ambiguity is not really typical of the stories of *Red Cavalry*.

So much, then, for "line." We know from Babel's diary that virtually every detail of *Red Cavalry* is based on actual observations.[18] Babel himself said that he lacked "fantasy."[19] The secret of his art, he said, lay in the way he reassembled the sundry scraps of a reality which was not in itself poetic. There are those who say it is essentially "style" that keeps Babel's stories together.[20] This may be too simple an answer. I think it is really composition, the details of which are different for every single story and practically for every single juncture.

I have already discussed "line." In a few stories suspense is a factor. Will Ivan Akinfiev kill the Deacon? Ironically, the story breaks off before the suspense is lifted. Will Konkin kill his prisoner? He does – as an afterthought, so to speak. But much more often suspense is momentary, a distinct, particulate entity – like images, gnomes, and rhetorical tirades. It comes and it goes, for instance, in "The Death of Dolgushov" or "After the Battle," where for a moment Liutov's life hangs in the balance.

By and large Babel's stories are examples of ideological disinterestedness. But a few times it seems there is an epiphany that casts light on the whole story. In "Sandy the Christ," I think the following passage is pivotal:

> "For the love of God, let me go, Tarakanych," Sandy begged once more. "All the saints used to be shepherds."
> "Sandy the Saint!" guffawed the stepfather. "Caught syphilis from the Mother of God."

It is this brief dialogue that establishes Sandy as a saint in travesty. It is not difficult to detect allegory in this, and in a few other stories. But I daresay that, once again, the allegory is a distinct motive rather than an element underlying the structure of the whole story.

There are a few lyric pieces in which lyric parallelism is the significant structural pattern ("The Road to Brody," "The Cemetery at Kozin"), and one or two where contrast seems to act as the structural pivot. In "The Song" the squalor of poverty is set against the beauty of a song. In "Berestechko" the reeking Jewish ghetto stands opposite a genteel French letter, and a Communist Party meeting takes place at the foot of the castle of Count Raciborski.

Yet by and large, and surely in most of the stories in *Red Cavalry*, the composition must be accounted for motive by motive, transition by transition. Such great stories as "Pan Apolek" or "The Rabbi's Son" are original compositions that cannot be reduced to any particular pattern, or even to any particular genre.

The Babelian short story at its best seems to realize that poetic balance between thought and image, line and color, movement and structure in a way that is characteristic of great lyric poetry.[21] The emphasis is on image, color, and structure, rather than on thought, line, and movement. Ehrenburg is quite right when he calls Babel a poet.[22] Such nonlyrical ingredients as philosophical abstraction, plot, irony, and rhetoric are transformed by him into concrete verbal units, small and light enough to float about in Babel's space of color. Babel also displays a healthy dose of that Goethian "narrowness, enamored of reality," which is proper to the true lyric poet. In many respects Babel's art in *Red Cavalry* resembles that of the acmeist-imaginist school of lyric poetry, in particular that of the great acmeist poet Osip Mandelstam.[23]

NOTES

1. See, e.g. Renato Poggioli, *The Phoenix and the Spider* (Cambridge, Mass.: Harvard University Press, 1957), p. 233; Marc Slonim, *Soviet Russian Literature: Writers and Problems* (New York: Oxford University Press, 1964), p. 70; and Gleb Struve, *Soviet Russian Literature* (Norman: Oklahoma University Press [c. 1951]), p. 67.

2. Lionel Trilling used the expression "lyric joy" in his introduction to Isaac Babel, *The Collected Stories* (New York: New American Library, 1960), p. 17.

3. Emil Staiger, *Grundbegriffe der Poetik* (Zürich: Atlantis, 1961), *passim*.

4. I am using the word *travesty* in the sense in which it appears in German as well as in French criticism, a sense that is closer to the etymological meaning of the word. *Travesty* in my usage here is "replacing (or distorting) the form of an original without, however, changing the content." *Parody*, accordingly, replaces (or distorts) the content of the original, while retaining the form.

5. The conception of the "picaresque saint," developed in R.W.B. Lewis's book *The Picaresque Saint: Representative Figures in Contemporary Fiction* (Philadelphia: Lippincott, 1959), is certainly pertinent here.

6. I am taking this conception from Gerhard Gesemann, *Heroische Lebensform, zur literatur und Wesenskunde der balkanischen Patriarchalität* (Berlin: Wirkung, 1943).

7. The Babelian conflict between "line" and "color" is observed, very clearly, by Heddy Pross-Weerth in her epilogue to Isaak Babel, *Sonnenun-*

tergang (Olten: Walter, 1962), p. 278. It fits beautifully into Heinrich Wölfflin's broad historical conception.

8. The prophetic nature of these words is pointed out by Rufus Matthewson, Jr., in *The Positive Hero in Russian Literature* (New York: Columbia University Press, 1958), p. 257.

9. Struve, p. 67.

10. See, e.g., Wolfgang Kayser, *Das sprachliche Kunstwerk* (Berlin, 1962), pp. 80–81, 179–180, 210–212, 338, 355.

11. Struve's felicitous comparison.

12. Babel is reported to have said: "A short story must have the precision of a military report or a bank check. It must be written in the same firm, direct hand one uses for orders and checks" (K. Paustovskii, *Vremia bol'shikh ozhidanii* [Moscow: Gos. izd-vo khudozh lit-ry, 1960], p. 127). An English translation of Paustovskii's reminiscences is found in *Partisan Review* 3 (1961), 391–415.

13. My translation from Paustovskii, *Vremia*, pp. 152–153.

14. I am taking this distinction between "composition" and "construction" from Leo Stein, *Appreciation: Painting, Poetry and Prose* (New York: Crown, 1947), pp. 48–49.

15. See Kayser, *Sprachliche Kunstwerk*, p. 71.

16. I do not know who was the first to point out this analogy. H. Pross-Weerth mentions it (p. 279) without giving a source.

17. Here I may be in slight disagreement with Matthewson, who says: "[skaz] is a device Babel frequently uses to effect those human exposures that are his main concern. It is the technique of the slow disclosure of a situation through the naive view of a participant who comprehends dimly (if at all) the consequences or meanings of what he is describing" (*Positive Hero*, p. 259). In my opinion the real point of the *skaz*-type stories lies in the exposure of the gaping chasm between the sensibility of the uneducated narrator and that of Babel himself. The rift is immediately patent in every case, although one may become more aware of its abysmal depth as the story proceeds.

18. See I. Ehrenburg, "Liudi, gody, zhizn'," *Novyi mir*, no. 9 (1961): 148–49.

19. Paustovskii, *Vremia*, p. 149.

20. Struve, among others, is of that opinion (*Soviet Russian Literature*, 66). See also Leonid Rzhevskii, "Babel'-stilist," *Vozdushnye puti* 3 (1963): 217–41.

134 : Criticism

21. I am following Theophil Spoerri's conception in *Der Weg zur Form* (Hamburg: Furche, 1954), pp. 23–24.

22. Ehrenburg, "Liudi, gody, zhizn'," p. 150.

23. Struve brings up the analogy with Imaginist poetry (*Soviet Russian Literature*, p. 67). See also J. van der Eng, "La description poétique chez Babel," in *Dutch Contributions to the Fifth International Congress of Slavicists, Sofia, 1963*, Slavistic Printings and Reprintings 45 (The Hague, 1963).

III   PRIMARY SOURCES

Selections from *1920 Diary*

The diary begins on page 55 of Babel's notebook; the first 54 pages are missing. [. . .] indicates elided text.

ZHITOMIR. 3 JUNE [JULY] 1920

Morning in the train, came for tunic and boots. I'm sleeping with Zhukov, Topolnik, it's filthy, morning sun in my eyes, railroad-car filth. Lanky Zhukov, gluttonous Topolnik, the whole editorial team – unbelievably filthy fellows.

Revolting tea in borrowed mess tins. Letters home, packets for YUGROSTA, interview with Pollak, operation to get control of Novograd, discipline in the Polish army is getting weaker, Polish White Guard literature, booklets of cigarette paper, matches, erstwhile (Ukrainian) Jews, commissars, all of it stupid, malicious, feeble, incompetent, and extraordinarily unconvincing. Mikhailov's extracts from Polish newspapers.

The kitchen on the train, fat soldiers with florid faces, gray souls, suffocating heat in the kitchen, kasha, midday, sweat, thick-legged washerwomen, phlegmatic creatures – lathes – describe the soldiers and the women, fat, overfed, sleepy.

Love in the kitchen.

After dinner to Zhitomir. White town, not sleepy, but battered, hushed. I look for traces of Polish culture. Women well-dressed, white stockings. Catholic church.

Bathe near Nuska in the Teterev, nasty little river, old Jewish men at the bathing place, their long skinny legs covered with gray hairs. Young Jews. Women washing clothes in the Teterev. A family – beautiful wife, husband carrying child.

Market in Zhitomir, old cobbler, blueing, whiting, shoelaces.

Synagogue buildings, ancient architecture, how deeply it all moves me.

Watch crystal 1,200 rubles. Market. A little Jew, a philosopher. Unimaginable Shop – Dickens, brooms and golden slippers. His philosophy – they all say they're fighting for justice and they all loot. If only some government or other were a kind one. Remarkable words, little beard, we talk, tea and three apple tarts – 750 rubles. [. . .]

Zhitomir pogrom, organized by the Poles, continued, of course, by the Cossacks.

When our advance troops appeared the Poles entered the town, stayed for 3 days, there was a pogrom, they cut off beards, that's usual, assembled 45 Jews in the marketplace, led them to the slaughteryard, tortures, cut out tongues, wails heard all over the square. They set fire to 6 houses, I went to look at Koniuchowski's house on Cathedral Street, they machine-gunned those who tried to rescue people. The yardman, into whose arms a mother dropped a child from a burning window, was bayoneted, the priest put a ladder up against the back wall, they escaped that way.

Sabbath waning, we go from the father-in-law's to see the tsaddik. I didn't get his name. A staggering picture for me, though the signs of dying and complete decadence are plain to see. The tsaddik himself – his broad-shouldered, emaciated figure. His son – a noble boy in a gaberdine, I could see petit-bourgeois but spacious rooms. All very sedate, wife an ordinary Jewish woman, even a little "moderne."

The faces of the old Jews.

Conversations in the corner about rising prices.

I can't find my place in the prayerbook. Podolsky puts me right.

No candle – a tallow dip instead.

I feel happy, enormous faces, hooked noses, black beards with a sprinkling of gray, I think about many things, good-bye, dead men. The tsaddik's face, his nickel-rimmed pince-nez.

"Where are you from, young man?"

"From Odessa."

"How is life there?"

"People live."

"And here it's a horror."

A short conversation.

I leave feeling shaken.

[...]

And then it's night, the train, painted over with communist slogans (contrast with what I saw among the old Jews).

The rattle of typewriters, our own generator, our own newspapers, a film showing, the train a blaze of light, its rumbling, fat-faced soldiers lining up for the washerwoman (a two-day wait).

BELYOV. 11 JULY 1920

[...]

I roam around the village. Go to Klevan, a town taken yesterday by 3rd Cavalry Brigade of 6th Division. [...]

Budyonny's orders about our loss of Rovno, about the incredible weariness of the troops, the fact that furious attacks by our brigades do not yield the same results as before, uninterrupted fighting since 27 May, if we aren't given a breathing space the army will become unfit to fight.

[...]

My first requisition – a notebook. The synagogue caretaker Menashe accompanies me. I eat at Mudrik's, same old story, the Jews have been plundered, their bewilderment, they expected the Soviet regime to liberate them, and suddenly there were shrieks, whips cracking, shouts of "dirty Yid."

[...]

Klevan, its roads, its streets, the peasants and communism far apart.

BELYOV. 13 JULY 1920

My birthday. I'm 26. Think about home, about my work, my life is flying by. No manuscripts. A dull misery, must get the better of it. I'm keeping my journal, that will be something interesting.

Handsome young clerks, young Russians on HQ staff sing arias from operettas, they're a bit spoiled by working at HQ. Describe the dispatch rider, those working for the divisional chief of staff, and the rest of them – Cherkashin, Tarasov, looters, lickspittles, sycophants, gluttons, idlers. The legacy of the past, they know who's master.

[. . .]

Dyakov, the remount officer – pantomime picture, red trousers with silver stripes, gold-embossed belt, from Stavropol, built like an Apollo, short gray moustache, 45, has a son and a nephew, fantastic oaths, they brought things from the supply department, he smashed a desk, but got what he wanted. Dyakov, the soldiers love him, our commander's a hero, was an athlete, barely literate, now "I'm Inspector of Cavalry," a general. Dyakov is a communist, brave, an old Budyonny man. Met a millionaire, with a lady on his arm – "tell me, Mr. Dyakov, haven't we met at the club?" "I've been in eight countries, when I take the stage I need only wink."

He's a dancer, concertina player, crafty, a tall-talker, most picturesque character. Has difficulty reading documents, keeps losing them, it's got me down, he says all this paperwork, if I give up where will they be without me, his swearing, the way he talks to the peasants, they listen openmouthed. [. . .]

BELYOV. 14 JULY 1920

[. . .]

Frank Mosher. American airman, shot down, barefoot but elegant, neck like a pillar, dazzlingly white teeth, clothes covered with oil and dirt. Asks me anxiously whether he's committed a crime, fighting against Soviet Russia. Our cause is strong. Ah, but all at once – the smell of Europe, its cafés, civilization, power, ancient culture, so many thoughts, I watch him, can't take my eyes off him. Letter from Major Fauntleroy – things bad in Poland, no constitution, Bolsheviks strong, socialists the center of attention but not in power. We must study the new methods of warfare. What are they telling Western European soldiers? Russian imperialism, they want to abolish nationhood, customs, that's the main thing – annex all the Slav lands, such antiquated words. Endless conversation with Mosher, I'm absorbed in old memories, they'll shake you up, Mosher, ah, Conan Doyle, letters to New York. Whether he's just putting on an act or not, Mosher is frantically eager to find out what Bolshevism is all about. Sad and delicious impression.

[. . .]

Divisional Commander Timoshenko at HQ. A colorful figure. A colossus in red half-leather trousers, red cap, well-built, former platoon commander, was at one time a machine gunner, an artillery ensign. Fabulous stories. The commissar of the 1st Brigade was afraid of fire, the lads mounted, he starts using his whip on the regimental commanders, including Kniga, he shoots at the commissar, to horse you bastards, charges at them, 5 shots, comrades, help, I'll show you, shoots himself through the hand, through one eye, the revolver jams, I gave the commissar a dressing-down, he electrifies the Cossacks, a Budyonny man – go up forward with him and if the Poles don't kill you, he will.

[. . .]

The village, deserted, a light at HQ, Jewish detainees. Budyonny's men bring communism, a woman weeps. Oh, what a dismal life Russians lead. What's become of Ukrainian gaiety? The harvest is beginning. Poppies are ripening, where can I get corn for the horses and cherry dumplings?

[. . .]

BELYOV. 15 JULY 1920

Interrogating deserters. They show us some of our own leaflets. They are very effective, these leaflets help the Cossacks.

[. . .]

We've captured a proclamation by Piłsudski – "Warriors of the Rzecz Pospolita." A moving proclamation. "Our graves are white with the bones of five generations of warriors, our ideals, our Poland, our shining home, the eyes of your homeland are on you, it trembles, our young freedom, one more effort, our thoughts are of you, all for you, soldiers of the Rzecz Pospolita."

Touching, sad, no iron Bolshevik arguments, no promises, and words like *order, ideals, live in freedom.* Our side is winning!

[. . .]

NOVOSELKI – MALYI DOROGOSTAI. 18 JULY 1920

[. . .]

An order comes from the Southwest Army Group: when we enter Galicia – the first time Soviet troops cross the frontier – we are to treat the population well. We are not entering a conquered country, the country belongs to the workers and peasants of Galicia, and to them alone, we are going there to help them establish Soviet rule. An important and sensible order, but will the scavengers obey it? No.

[. . .]

The Jewish cemetery outside Malin, hundreds of years old, grave-stones have toppled over, almost all the same shape, oval at the top, the cemetery is overgrown with grass, it has seen Khmelnitsky, now Budyonny, unfortunate Jewish population, everything repeats itself, now that whole story – Poles, Cossacks, Jews – is repeating itself with stunning exactitude, the only new element is communism.

[. . .]

With the Cossacks when they stop for a rest, hay for the horses, every one of them has a long story to tell – Denikin, farmsteads of their own, their own leaders, the Budyonnys and the Knigas, cam-paigns with 200 men, bandit raids, the rich, free Cossack life, how many officers' heads they've cut off. They read the newspaper, but the names don't sink in, it's so easy to get everything turned around.

Splendid comradeship, solidarity, love of horses, a Cossack's horse occupies a quarter of his day, endless bartering, arguments. The role and life of the horse.

Their behavior toward their superiors is quite unique – simple, familiar.

[. . .]

MALYI DOROGOSTAI – SMORDVA – BEREZHTSY.
19 JULY 1920

[. . .]
I feel worse and worse. My temperature is 39.8. Budyonny and Voroshilov arrive.

Conference. The div. commander flies past. The battle begins. I lie in the priest's garden. Grishchuk is completely apathetic. What Grishchuk is like: submissive, eternally quiet, infinitely sluggish. He's fifty versts from home, hasn't been there in six years, and doesn't run away.

He knows what obeying your superiors means, the Germans taught him.

The wounded start coming in, bandages, bare bellies, long-suffering, unbearable heat, shot at from both sides, no letup, impossible to doze off. Budyonny and Voroshilov on the porch, battle picture, the cavalry return, dust-stained, sweating, red-faced, no trace of excitement after their butcher's work, professionals, it's all done perfectly calmly – that's what makes them special, their self-assurance, hard work, nurses on horseback gallop by, an armored car.

[. . .]

21 JULY 1920. PELCHA – BORATYN

We have taken Dubno. The resistance, whatever we say, was minimal. Why? Prisoners tell us, and we can see for ourselves – a revolution of the little people. There's a lot you could say about it, the beauty of the Polish facade, there is something touching about it all, my countess. Fate, Polish honor, the Jews, Count Ledochowski. Proletarian revolution. How eagerly I breathe in the scent of Europe – blowing from out there.

[. . .]
A beautiful day. My interview with Konstantin Karlovich. What sort of person is our Cossack? Many-layered: looting, reckless daring, professionalism, revolutionary spirit, bestial cruelty. We are the

vanguard, but of what? The population await their saviors, the Jews look for liberation – and in ride the Kuban Cossacks.

The army commander summons the divisional commander to Kozin for consultation. 7 versts away. I go with him. Sands. Every house remains in my heart. Clusters of Jews. Their faces – this is the ghetto, and we are an ancient people, exhausted, but we still have some strength left, a shop, I drink splendid coffee, I pour balm on the soul of the shopkeeper, who is listening to the noise in his shop. Cossacks yelling, swearing, climbing over the shelves, too bad for the shop, sweating, ginger-bearded Jew. I wander around endlessly, can't tear myself away, the town was destroyed, is rebuilding, has existed four hundred years, remains of a synagogue, magnificent old temple in ruins, what was a Catholic and is now an Orthodox church, en-chantingly white, with triple door, visible from afar, now Orthodox. An old Jew – I like talking with my own kind – they understand me. Cemetery, Rabbi Azrael's ruined house, three generations, the grave-stone under a tree that has grown up over it, those old stones, all the same shape, with the same message, this exhausted Jew who is my guide, a family of stupid-looking, thick-legged Jews living in a wooden shed by the cemetery, graves of three Jewish soldiers, killed in the Russo-German war. The Abramoviches from Odessa, the mother came for the burial, and I can see this Jewish woman, bury-ing a son killed in battle for a cause which to her is revolting, incomprehensible, criminal.

An old and a new cemetery – the town is four hundred years old.

Evening, I walk around among the houses, Jewish men and women reading posters and proclamations, "Poland is the running dog of the bourgeoisie" and so on. "Insects can kill" and "do not remove stoves from heated boxcars."

These Jews are like portraits, elongated, silent, long-bearded, not like our type, fat and jovial. Lofty old men, hanging around with nothing to do. Most important – the shop and the cemetery.

Back seven versts to Boratyn, beautiful evening, my heart is full, rich householders, pert girls, fried eggs, fatback, our soldiers catching flies, the Russo-Ukrainian soul. I'm not sure I'm really interested.

23 JULY 1920. BORATYN

[. . .]

Dubno synagogues. Everything destroyed. Two little vestibules left, centuries, two tiny rooms, everything full of memories, four synagogues, close together, then pasture, plowed fields, the setting sun. The synagogues are ancient buildings, squat, green and blue, the Hasidic synagogue, inside, nondescript architecture. I go into the Hasidic synagogue. It's Friday. Such misshapen little figures, such worn faces, it all came alive for me, what it was like three hundred years ago, the old men running about the synagogue, no wailing, for some reason they keep moving from corner to corner, their worship could not be less formal. Of all the Jews in Dubno the most repulsive looking seem to have gathered here. I pray, or rather almost pray, thinking of Hershele and how to describe him. A quiet evening in the synagogue, that always has an irresistible effect on me, four synagogues in a row. Religion? There are no adornments in the building, everything is white and plain to the point of asceticism, everything is fleshless, bloodless, to a grotesque degree, you have to have the soul of a Jew to sense what it means. But what does the soul consist of? Can it be that ours is the century in which they perish?

[. . .]

24 JULY 1920

Morning – at army HQ. 6th Division is mopping up the enemy attacking us in Khotin, the battle zone is between Khotin and Kozin, and I think, unlucky Kozin.

Cemetery, rounded gravestones.

Ride with Prishchepa from Krivikha to Leszniów via Demidovka. Prishchepa's soul – an illiterate boy, a communist, parents killed by Kadets, tells how he went round the village collecting his property. A picturesque figure with his hood, as simple as a blade of grass, will be a looter, despises Grishchuk because he doesn't like or understand horses.

[. . .]

Prishchepa, restrained by me for quite a while, finally breaks out
– fucking Yids, the whole arsenal of abuse, they all, hating us and
me, go and dig potatoes, afraid in someone else's garden, they blame
crosses, Prishchepa seethes. How excruciating it all is – Artsybashev, the orphaned schoolgirl from Rovno, Prishchepa in his
hood. The mother wrings her hands – a fire lit on the Sabbath, bad
language flying around. Budyonny has been here and left. Argument between a Jewish youth and Prishchepa. The youth wears
glasses, is dark-haired, nervous, has scarlet inflamed eyelids, speaks
Russian incorrectly. He believes in God, says God is an ideal we
carry in our souls, every person has in his soul his own God, if you
behave badly God grieves – this foolishness is pronounced in an
exalted fashion and as if it hurt. Prishchepa is insultingly stupid, he
goes on about religion in antiquity, confuses Christianity and paganism, his main point is that in antiquity there were communes, of
course, he babbles incoherently, says your education is nonexistent,
and the Jew has gone through sixth form at the Rovno gymnasium –
he parrots Platonov, it's touching and comic – clans, clan elders,
Perun, paganism.

We eat like oxen, fried potatoes and five tumblersful of coffee
each. We sweat, they keep serving us, all this is terrible, I tell them
fairy tales about Bolshevism – the blossoming, the express trains,
Moscow's textile mills, universities, free meals, the Revel delegation,
to crown it all the story of the Chinese, and I captivate all these
tormented people. It's the 9th of Av. The old woman sobs, sitting on
the floor, and her son, who worships his mother and says he believes
in God just to please her, sings in a pleasant, light tenor, and tells the
story of the destruction of the Temple. The terrible words of the
prophet – they eat dung, their maidens are ravished, their menfolk
killed, Israel subjugated, words of wrath and sorrow. The lamp
smokes, the old woman wails, the young man sings melodiously, girls
in white stockings, outside – Demidovka, night, Cossacks, all just as
it was when the Temple was destroyed. I go out to sleep in the yard,
stinking and damp.

26 JULY 1920. LESZNIÓW

The Ukraine is in flames. Wrangel has not been liquidated. Makhno is making raids in Yekaterinoslav and Poltava provinces. New robber gangs have appeared, there is an uprising in the Kherson region. Why are they rebelling, doesn't the communist jacket fit?

[. . .]

The life of our division. About Bahturov, about the div. commander, about the Cossacks, the looting, the avant-garde of the avant-garde. I am an outsider.

29 JULY 1920. LESZNIÓW

[. . .]

Galicia is intolerably dreary, battered churches and calvaries, overcast sky, cowed, mediocre, insignificant population. Pitiful people, habituated to all the killing, to soldiers, to disorder, matronly Russian women in tears, rutted roads, stunted grain crops, no sun, Catholic priests with broad hats – but without churches. Deep depression emanates from all those trying to make themselves some sort of life.

The Slavs – the manure of history?

[. . .]

30 JULY 1920. BRODY

[. . .]

The town has been wrecked, looted. A town of immense interest. Polish culture. An ancient, rich idiosyncratic Jewish settlement. These horrible markets, dwarves in gaberdines, gaberdines and peyes, old, old men. School Street, nine synagogues, all half-destroyed, I inspect the new synagogue, architecture [two words indecipherable], the shammes, a bearded and talkative Jew – if only there were peace, how good business would be, tells me how the

Cossacks plundered the town, the humiliations inflicted by the Poles.

[. . .]

The highway, barbed wire, felled trees, and the dreariness, the everlasting dreariness. Nothing to eat, nothing to rely on, war, they're all as bad as the other, equally alien, hostile, savage, where once life was quiet and, most important, replete with tradition.

[. . .]

31 JULY 1920. BRODY, LESZNIÓW

This morning, before leaving, with the tachanka waiting on Golden Street, an hour in a bookshop, a German shop. All sorts of magnificent uncut books, albums, the West, here you have the West, and chivalrous Poland, a chrestomathy, the history of all the Boleslaws, and something tells me that this beauty, this Poland, is so many glittering garments draped around a decrepit body. I rummage among the books like a madman, skim here and there, it's dark, a crowd pours in to loot the stationer's, loathsome young men from the Commission for Captured Enemy Property, with an exaggeratedly martial air. I tear myself away from the shop in despair.

[. . .]

1 AUGUST 1920. GRZYMAŁÓWKA, LESZNIÓW

God, it's August, we shall die soon, the ineradicable cruelty of human beings.

[. . .]

The battle outside Leszniów. Our infantry in trenches, it's remarkable, young lads from Volhynia, barefoot, semi-idiotic – Russian peasants, and they are actually fighting against Poles, against the gentlemen oppressors.

[. . .]

The day is over, I have seen death, white roads, horses under the trees, sunrise and sunset. Above all – Budyonny's men, their horses,

troop movements and war, grave, barefoot, spectral Galicians walking through the wheat fields.

[...]

2 AUGUST 1920. BILAWCE

[...]

I'm tired. Alarm at HQ. We are pulling out. The enemy is putting
the pressure on.

[...]

I am assigned a field ambulance belonging to the 2nd Squadron,
we ride up to the forest, halt there with Ivan, my driver. Budyonny
and Voroshilov arrive, this will be the decisive battle, not a single
step farther.

[...]

We wander about the fields for ages, under fire, can't see a thing,
these uncaring roads, this scrubby grass, we send out riders, come
out onto the highway – where to next, Radziwiłłow or Brody?

[...]

. . . we head for Radziwiłłow. We arrive in the night. . . . I choose
a cottage on the outskirts . . . . machine-gun fire, clatter of wagons,
we rush out, the horse has developed a limp, that's the way it goes,
we flee in panic, we are fired on, we can't understand what's happening, he'll catch us any minute now, we charge onto the bridge,
milling hordes, we slip into the bog, wild panic, a dead man lying
there, abandoned carts, shells, tachankas. Traffic jam, night, terror,
wagons at a standstill, endless lines of them, we move on, stop, sleep,
stars. What I feel worst about in this whole business is the tea I was
deprived of, feel so bad that it seems strange to me. I think about this
all night, and hate war.

What a troubled life.

3 AUGUST 1920

Night in an open field, we are moving toward Brody in a wag-
onette. The town keeps changing hands. The same horrifying pic-

ture, half in ruins, and the town is waiting for it to happen again.

[. . .]

The battlefield, I meet the div. commander, where is HQ staff, we have lost Zholnarkevich. The battle begins, artillery cover, explosions quite near, a fearful moment, the decisive battle – will we halt the Polish advance or won't we, Budyonny to Kolesnikov and Grishin – "I'll shoot you," they go away white-faced, on foot.

Before that – the dreadful field, sown with mangled men, inhuman cruelty, unbelievable wounds, fractured skulls, naked young bodies gleaming white in the sun, jettisoned notebooks, leaflets, soldiers' books, Bibles, bodies among the wheat.

[. . .]

The beginning of my adventures, I make for the highway with the supply wagons, the fighting gets fiercer, I find a provisioning point under fire on the highway, shells whistling past, explosions twenty paces away, felling of hopelessness, the wagons leave at a gallop, I tag on to the 20th Regiment, 4th Division, wounded men, cantankerous commander, no, he says, I'm not wounded, just got a knock, we're professionals, and nothing but fields, sun, corpses, I sit by the field kitchen, hunger, dried peas, no fodder for the horses.

[. . .]

An apiary, we search the hives, four huts in the forest, nothing there, everything stolen, I ask a Red Army man for bread, he says "I don't have anything to do with Jews," I'm an outsider, in long trousers, I don't belong, I'm all alone, we ride on, I'm so tired I can hardly sit on my horse, I have to look after it myself, we ride into Koniuszków, we steal some barley, they tell me to look around and take what I can, take the lot, I look around the village for a nurse, women in hysterics, five minutes after our arrival the looting starts, women struggling, weeping and wailing, it's unbearable, I can't stand these never-ending horrors, I go looking for a nurse, I feel unbearably sad, I pinch a mug of milk from the regimental commander, snatch a flatcake out of the hands of a peasant woman's little boy.

[. . .]

5 AUGUST 1920. KHOTIN

[. . .]

. . . Apanasenko, a new and striking figure, ugly, uncouth, hot-headed, egotistical, ambitious, appealed to Stavropol and the Don about disorder in the rear, just to let his native place know that he is a div. commander. Timoshenko was easier, jollier, more broad-minded, and perhaps worse. . . .

[. . .]

7 AUGUST 1920. BERESTECHKO

[. . .]

A memorable day. In the morning – from Khotin to Berestechko.

[. . .]

Corpse of a murdered Pole, a terrifying corpse, swollen and naked, grotesque.

Berestechko has changed hands several times. Historic fields outside Berestechko, Cossack graves. The most striking thing is how everything repeats itself – Cossack against Pole, more often still – peasant against Polish landlord.

I won't forget this town with its long, narrow, roofed-in stinking courtyards, all of it 100–200 years old, its population sturdier than in other places, above all, the architecture, white and watery-blue little houses, lanes, synagogues, peasant women. Life is slowly returning to normal. Life here used to be worth living, a solid Jewish community, rich Ukrainians, market on Sundays, a unique class of Russian urban artisans, leather workers, trade with Austria, smuggling.

The Jews here are less fanatical, better dressed, more robust, you could even say jollier, very old men, gaberdines, old women, everything is redolent of olden times, tradition, the town is steeped in the bloody history of the Polish-Jewish ghetto. Hatred for the Poles is unanimous. They have looted, tortured, branded the pharmacist with a red-hot iron, put needles under his nails, pulled out his hair, all because someone shot at a Polish officer. What idiocy. The Poles have gone mad, they are destroying themselves.

An ancient Catholic church, graves of Polish officers in the churchyard, fresh mounds, ten days old, birchwood crosses, all this is horrible, the priest's house has been destroyed, I find ancient books, precious Latin manuscripts. The priest was called Tuzinkiewicz. I find a photograph of him, short and fat, labored here 45 years, lived in the same place, a scholastic, a varied collection of books, many in Latin. 1860 editions, that's when Tuzinkiewicz really lived, huge old-fashioned living quarters, dark pictures, photographs of church dignitaries assembled in Zhitomir, portraits of Pope Pius X, a nice face, an amazing portrait of Sienkiewicz – there he is, the essence of a nation.

[. . .]

A dreadful incident, the church was sacked, vestments torn up, precious, shimmering fabrics in tatters, on the floor, the nurse made off with three bales, linings were ripped open, candles stolen, chests staved in, papal bulls thrown out, money pocketed, a magnificent church, 200 years old, the things it's seen (Tuzinkiewicz's manuscripts), so many counts and serfs, magnificent Italian paintings, rosy priests rocking the infant Christ, a magnificent dark Christ, Rembrandt, a Madonna in the manner of Murillo, maybe it is a Murillo, and above all those well-nourished, saintly Jesuits, an eerie, miniature Chinese figure behind a veil, wearing a raspberry-colored Polish frock coat, a bearded little Jew, a bench, a shattered shrine, the statue of St. Valentine. The verger quivers like a bird, writhes, speaks a mixture of Russian and Polish, I'm not allowed to touch it he sobs. "They're wild beasts, they've come to wreck and rob, it's obvious, the old gods are being destroyed."

Evening in the town. The church is closed. In the late afternoon I visit the castle of the counts Raciborowski. An old man of 70 and his 90-year-old mother. There were just the two of them, both mad, so the locals say. Describe this pair. Ancient, aristocratic Polish house, probably more than 100 years old, bright, old-fashioned paintings on the ceilings, remains of antlers, small rooms for the servants up above, flagstones, passageways, excrement on the floor, little Jewish boys, a Steinway piano, sofas ripped open, springs sticking out, remember the doors, light white doors, oak doors, letters in French dated 1820, "notre petit héros achève 7 semaines." God who can have written them, and when, these trampled letters, I pick up some relics, a century ago, the mother a countess, a Steinway, the park, an artificial lake.

I can't tear myself away – I think of Hauptmann, of Elga.

Public meeting in the castle park, the Jews of Berestechko, obtuse Vinokurov, children running around, a Revolutionary Committee is being elected, the Jewish men finger their beards, Jewish women listen to what's said about the Russian paradise, the international situation, the rising in India.

[. . .]

8 AUGUST 1920. BERESTECHKO

[. . .]

I am lodging with the proprietress of an inn, a skinny redheaded old bag. Ilchenko has bought some cucumbers, is reading *Everybody's Magazine* and holding forth on economic policy, says the Jews are to blame for everything, an obtuse Slav creature, stuffed his pockets when Rostov was sacked. Some foster children, mother recently dead. The story of the pharmacist, the Poles stuck pins under his fingernails, insane people.

[. . .]

Moscow newspapers dated 29 July. Opening of the Second Congress of the Third International, unification of the peoples finally realized, now all is clear: there are two worlds, and war between them is declared. We will fight on endlessly. Russia has thrown down the gauntlet. We shall advance into Europe and conquer the world. The Red Army has become a factor of world significance.

Must take a closer look at Apanasenko. An ataman.

[. . .]

10 AUGUST 1920. ŁASZKÓW

[. . .]

Our Cossacks, a depressing spectacle, stealing things from the back porch, their eyes smarting, all looking sheepish, it's ineradicable, this so-called force of habit. . . .

[. . .]

Night – an unusual spectacle, the highroad burning brightly in the last rays, my room is lit up, I'm working, the lamp is lit, peace and quiet, the Kuban Cossacks are singing sentimentally, their slim forms in the light of camp fires, the songs are just like Ukrainian ones, the horses lie down to sleep. I go to the div. commander's. I hear stories about him from Vinokurov – a partisan, an ataman, a rebel, Cossack freedom, a wild uprising, his ideal is Dumenko, an open wound, must subordinate yourself to an organization, deadly hatred of the aristocracy, the priests and, above all, the intelligentsia, whose presence in the army he can't stomach. He'll graduate from an institute – Apanasenko, how is it different from the times of Bogdan Khmelnitsky?

Middle of the night. 4 A.M.

11 AUGUST 1920. ŁASZKÓW

[. . .]

Apanasenko is hungry for fame, here it is – the new class. Whatever the battle plans – he breaks away and is back where he started, an organizer of task forces, simply hostile to officers, 4 George Crosses, a martinet, NCO, ensign in Kerensky's time, chairman of the regimental committee, stripped officers of their epaulets, long months in the Astrakhan steppes, incontestable authority, a professional soldier.

About the atamans, there were many of them around, they got hold of machine guns, fought with Shkuro and Mamontov, merged with the Red Army, a heroic epic. This isn't a Marxist revolution, it's a Cossack rebellion, out to win all and lose nothing. Apanasenko's hatred of the rich, of the intelligentsia, an unquenchable hatred.

Night with the Kuban Cossacks, rain, stuffy, I have some sort of peculiar itch.

18 AUGUST 1920

[. . .]

A whole volume could be written on women in the Red Army. The squadrons go into battle, dust, din, bared sabers, furious cursing, and they gallop forward with their skirts tucked up, covered in dust, with their big breasts, all whores, but comrades, whores because they're comrades, that's what matters, they're there to serve everybody, in any way they can, heroines, and at the same time despised, they water the horses, tote hay, mend harness, steal from the churches and from the civilian population.

[. . .]

I must look deeply into the soul of the fighting man, I am trying to, but it's all horrible, wild beasts with principles.

[. . .]

We spend the night in Zadworze, poor quarters, . . . I'm often at the observation point, the batteries at work, the forest fringes, hollows, machine guns mowing people down, the Poles are defending themselves mainly with aeroplanes, they're becoming a menace, describe an air attack, the distant, deceptively slow rattle of a machine gun, panic in the wagon trains, nerve-racking, they glide overhead incessantly, we hide from them. A new use of aviation, I think of Mosher, Captain Fauntleroy is in Lvov, our peregrination from one brigade to another, Kniga – only flanking movements, Kolesnikov – frontal attack, Sheko and I ride out to reconnoiter, unbroken forest, deadly danger, on the hills, bullets hum around us before the attack, Sukhorukov with a pitiful look on his face and a saber, I tag along behind the staff, we are waiting for reports, but they keep going, taking roundabout ways.

[. . .]

26 AUGUST 1920. SOKAL

Look around the town with the young Zionist. . . . The Jews ask me to use my influence to save them from ruin, they are being robbed of food and goods.

The Yids hide everything. The cobbler, the Sokal cobbler, is a proletarian. His apprentice's appearance – the redheaded Hasid is a cobbler.

The cobbler had looked forward to Soviet rule – and what he sees are Jew-baiters and looters, and that he won't be earning anything, he is dismayed and looks at us mistrustfully. Confusion over money. Strictly speaking we pay nothing, 15–20 rubles. The Jewish quarter. Indescribable poverty, filth, the seclusion of the ghetto.

[. . .]

When night comes the whole town will be looted – everybody knows it.

[. . .]

28 AUGUST 1920. KOMARÓW

[. . .]

The pharmacist, offering me a room. Rumor of atrocities. I walk into town. Indescribable terror and despair.

They tell me all about it. Privately, indoors, they're afraid the Poles may come back. Captain Yakovlev's Cossacks were here yesterday. A pogrom. The family of David Zys, in people's homes, a naked, barely breathing prophet of an old man, an old woman butchered, a child with fingers chopped off, many people still breathing, stench of blood, everything turned upside down, chaos, a mother sitting over her sabered son, an old woman lying twisted up like a pretzel, four people in one hovel, filth, blood under a black beard, just lying there in their blood. The Jews on the square, an agonized Jew showing it all to me, a tall Jew takes over from him. The rabbi hid, his whole house was taken apart, he waited till evening to creep out of his hole. 15 people killed, the Hasid Itska Galer, aged 70, David Zys, the synagogue caretaker, 45, his wife, his daughter, aged 15, David Trost and his wife – the ritual slaughterer.

At the home of a rape victim.

[. . .]

At night, a walk around the town.

Moonlight, their life at night, behind closed doors. Wailing beyond those walls. They'll clean it all up. The fear and horror of the inhabitants. The worst of it is – our men nonchalantly walk around looting wherever possible, stripping mangled corpses.

The hatred is the same, the Cossacks just the same, the cruelty the same, it's nonsense to think one army is different from another. The life of these little towns. There's no salvation. Everyone destroys them – the Poles gave them no refuge. The girls and women, all of them, can scarcely walk. In the evening – a talkative Jew with a little beard, used to keep a shop, daughter threw herself out of a second-story window to escape a Cossack, broke her arms, one of many.

What a mighty and marvelous life of a nation existed here. The fate of Jewry. At our place in the evening, supper, tea, I sit and drink in the words of the Jew with the little beard, wistfully asking me whether it will be possible to trade.

An oppressive, uneasy night.

30 AUGUST 1920

Morning – we leave Pniowek. The drive on Zamość continues. The weather is as horrible as ever, rain, slush, roads impassable, practically no sleep, on the floor, on straw, in our boots – must be prepared.

More hanging around. Sheko and I ride over to the 3rd Brigade. He goes to attack Zawady station, revolver in hand. Lepin and I stay in the forest. Lepin in agonies. The battle at the station. Sheko has a do-or-die look. Describe "rapid fire." We've taken the station. We ride up to the railroad track. Ten prisoners, we are too late to save one of them. Revolver wound? An officer. Bleeding from the mouth. Thick red blood, clotted, inundates his face, his face is horrible, red,

covered with a thick coating of blood. The prisoners are all undressed. The squadron commander has a pair of breeches slung over
his saddle. Sheko makes him give them back. They try to make the
prisoners dress, they won't. Officer's service cap. "There were nine
of them." Filthy language all around them. The men want to kill
them. Bald-headed, lame Jew in his undershorts, couldn't keep up
with his horse, terrible face, probably an officer, gets on everybody's
nerves, can't walk, all of them in a state of animal terror, pitiful,
unfortunate people, Polish proletarians, another Pole, stately, com-
posed, with side whiskers, wearing a knitted sweater, dignified demeanor, they keep asking whether he's an officer. The men want to
butcher them. A storm gathers over the Jew. A furious Putilov
worker says we ought to kill the lot of them, the bastards, the Jew
hops along behind us, we drag prisoners with us all the time, then
hand them over to the authority of escort troops. What will become
of them? The Putilov worker's fury, foaming at the mouth, sword
out, I'll cut the bastards up, and I won't have to answer for it.

[. . .]

31 AUGUST 1920. CZEŚNIKI

[. . .]

Budyonny says nothing, smiles occasionally, showing his dazzling
white teeth. A brigade must be sent in first, then a regiment. Voroshilov can't wait, he sends in everyone he's got. The regiment
parades for Voroshilov and Budyonny. Voroshilov pulls out an enormous revolver – show the Polish gents no mercy, his harangue is
received with approval. The regiment rushes out in disorder, hurrah,
let them have it, one gallops, another keeps a tight rein, a third is
trotting, the horses won't go, mess tins and carpet cloth. Our squadron joins the attack. We gallop about 4 versts. They're waiting for us
on the hill, drawn up in columns. Amazing – not one man budges.
Steadfastness, discipline. An officer with a black beard. I am being
fired at. My sensations. Flight. The military commissars try to turn

the fleeing men. Nothing helps. Fortunately the enemy doesn't pursue, otherwise there would be a catastrophe. Our side try to reassemble the brigade for a second attack, but without success. Manuilov is threatened with revolvers. Our only heroes are heroines – the nurses.

[. . .]

. . . Dismal prospects ahead.

1 SEPTEMBER 1920. TEREBIN

[. . .]

Beginning of the end for the 1st Cavalry Army. Talk of a retreat.

[. . .]

6 SEPTEMBER 1920. BUDYATICHI

Budyatichi occupied by 44th Division. Clashes. They were taken aback by the wild horde rushing in on them. Orlov – hand it over and get out.

A nurse, a proud, dim-witted, beautiful nurse in tears, a doctor outraged by yells of "Smash the Yids, save Russia!" They are stunned, the quartermaster has been thrashed with a whip, the contents of the clinic tossed out, pigs requisitioned and dragged off without receipt – and they had things in order, all sorts of plenipotentiaries visit Sheko with complaints. That's Budyonny's warriors for you.

[. . .]

My thoughts of home are more and more insistent. I cannot see where it will end.

7 SEPTEMBER 1920. BUDYATICHI

[. . .]

For two weeks now they've been talking more and more emphatically about the need to pull the army out for a rest. Let's rest – that's our battle cry!

[. . .]

12 SEPTEMBER 1920. KIVERTSY

In the morning – panic at the railroad station. Artillery fire. The Poles are in the town. Unimaginably wretched flight, . . .

[. . .]

. . . Shameful panic, an army incapable of fighting. Types of soldiers. The Russian Red Army infantryman, not just unmodernized, but the personification of "pauper Russia," wayfaring tramps, unhealthily swollen, bug-ridden, scrubby, half-starved peasants.

At Goloby the sick, the wounded, and the deserters are all thrown off the train. Rumors, afterward confirmed: the supply column of the 1st Cavalry Army, sent into the Vladimir-Volynsk cul-de-sac, has been seized by the enemy, our HQ has transferred to Lutsk, the 12th Army has lost a great number of men taken prisoner, a great deal of equipment, the whole army is on the run.

[. . .]

[The diary breaks off a few brief entries later, on 15 September.]

NOTES

The above selections are from *1920 Diary*, translated by H. T. Willetts, edited and with an introduction by Carol J. Avins (New Haven: Yale University Press, 1995), and appear by kind permission of Yale University Press. Many of the notes below are based on Avins's commentary.

3 June [July]: *Date:* As was noted in the Introduction, Babel could not have been in Zhitomir on 3 June, as the city was at that time held by the Poles. It probably should read 3 July. *Zhitomir:* City (1926 pop. 68,280) some eighty miles west-southwest of Kiev. An important center of Jewish intellectual life. Large-scale pogroms were perpetrated here by the Ukrainians in 1919 and by the Poles and the Russians in 1920. *Zhukov, Topolnik:* Fellow correspondents for *The Red Cavalryman*. *Pollak:* Staff officer of the Sixth Division. *Love in the kitchen:* See the story "Evening." *A little Jew, a philosopher:* See the story "Gedali." *Tsaddik:* A Hasidic leader recognized for his spiritual guidance and wisdom. See the stories "The Rabbi" ("The Rebbe") and "The Rabbi's Son" ("The Rebbe's Son"). *Soldiers lining up for the washerwoman:* See the story "Evening."

11 July: *Belyov, Klevan*: Villages about 9 miles northwest of Rovno.

13 July: *Dyakov*: See the story "The Remount Officer."

14 July: *Frank Mosher*: An alias used by Captain Merian C. Cooper of Jacksonville, Florida, who was instrumental in forming the Kosciuszko Squadron, a unit of mainly American pilots commanded by Cedric E. Faunt leroy who fought on the Polish side. Cooper spent several months in Soviet prisons before escaping. See the story "Squadron Commander Trunov." *Grishchuk*: See "The Death of Dolgushov" and "Discourse on the Tachanka." *Timoshenko*: Commander of the Sixth Division until early August. The model for Savitsky in "My First Goose" and "The Story of a Horse." *Kniga*: Commander of the First Brigade of the Second Division. See "The Brigade Commander."

15 July: *Piłsudski, Józef*: President of Poland and commander in chief of the army during the Russo-Polish war. *Rzech pospolita*: Republic (Polish). See the story "The Church at Novograd."

18 July: *The Jewish cemetery*: See the story "The Cemetery at Kozin," which contains similar reflections. *Khmelnitsky, Bogdan*: Sixteenth-century Cossack leader who led a rebellion against Polish rule that brought Ukraine under Russian control. He is famous for his massacre of many Jews.

19 July: *Voroshilov, Klement Efremovich*: Commissar of the First Cavalry Army, later Field Marshal and member of the Politburo. See the story "Chesniki."

21 July: *Konstantin Karlovich (Zholnarkevich)*: The staff commander. *Kozin*: A village whose population was 50% Jewish. See the story "The Cemetery at Kozin."

23 July: *Verba*: See the story "Two Ivans." *Dubno*: Pop. 9,146 (1921); 58% Jews. One of the oldest and most important Jewish centers in eastern Europe. *Hershele*: A trickster from Yiddish folklore. See Babel's 1918 story "Shabbos-Nachamu."

24 July: *Prishchepa*: See the story "Prishchepa's Vengeance." *Kadets*: The Constitutional Democratic Party, a liberal prerevolutionary party led by Pavel Milyukov that opposed Bolshevism. *Artsybashev, Mikhail Petrovich*: A prolific second-rate writer known especially for his novel *Sanin* (1907),

which reflected the themes of violence, cynicism, and debauchery popular in early twentieth-century Russia. *9th of Av*: The ninth day of the Hebrew month of Av, a date commemorating the destruction of the two Temples in Jerusalem (586 B.C. and 70 A.D.).

26 July: *Wrangel, Pyotr Nikolaevich*: White Russian general. His defeat in the Crimea in 1921 marked the end of the civil war. *Makhno, Nestor Ivanovich*: Peasant leader of the anarchist movement in Ukraine. *Bakhturov, P. V.*: Military commissar of the Sixth Division.

30 July: *Brody*: 1921 pop. 10,867. A center of the Berlin Enlightenment (Haskalah) movement in Galicia. See the story "The Road to Brody." *Peyes*: Sidelocks worn by Orthodox Jewish males. *Shammes*: Synagogue sexton.

31 July: *Boleslaws*: Polish royal dynasty that ruled from 992 until the thirteenth century.

3 August: *Kolesnikov*: Brigade commander in the Third Division. See the story "The Brigade Commander." *An apiary*: See the story "The Road to Brody."

5 August: *Apanasenko, Iosif Rodionovich*: Replaced Timoshenko as commander of the Sixth Division. The model for Pavlichenko in "The Life and Adventures of Matthew Pavlichenko."

7 August: *Berestechko*: Pop. 5,633 (1921). Scene of a battle on 28–30 June 1651, in which Bogdan Khmelnitsky's Cossacks were defeated by the Poles. See the story "Berestechko." *A dreadful incident*: See the story "In St. Valentine's Church." *The castle of the counts Raciborowski; "notre petit héros"*: See the story "Berestechko." *Hauptmann; Elga*: *Elga* is a play, set in a Polish monastery, by the German writer Gerhardt Hauptmann. *Obtuse Vinokurov*: Commissar. The model for Vinogradov in "Berestechko." *Rising in India*: A reference to Gandhi.

8 August: *Everybody's Magazine*: *Zhurnal dlya vsekh*. A popular illustrated Petersburg periodical (1896–1909).

10 August: *Dumenko, Boris Mokeevich*: Cossack cavalry commander and war hero.

11 August: *Kerensky, Aleksandr Fyodorovich*: Russian political leader; head of the Provisional Government at the time of the Bolshevik revolution. *Shkuro and Mamontov*: White cavalry commanders.

18 August: *Sheko, Ya. B.*: Staff commander. *Describe an air attack*: See the story "Squadron Commander Trunov."

26 August: *Sokal*: Pop. 10, 183. A Zionist center. See the story "Squadron Commander Trunov."

30 August: *"There were nine of them."* The title of a story Babel write in 1923 but never included in *Red Cavalry*. The incident described here is reflected in "Squadron Commander Trunov." *A furious Putilov worker*: The Putilov Works in St. Petersburg was one of the largest metallurgical and machine-building in Russia. Its workers were among the most ardent supporters of the Bolsheviks.

31 August: *Czésniki*: See the stories "Chesniki" and "After the Battle."

6 September: *Budyatichi*: See the story "The Song."

IV ❄ SELECT BIBLIOGRAPHY

Select Bibliography

Editions of *Red Cavalry* in Russian

Konarmiia. 3d revised edition. Moscow-Leningrad: Gos. izd-vo, 1928.
Flegon reprint (undated).
> Last of the "prerevised" editions of the work. With the
> exception of the 1979/1989 Jerusalem edition and this reprint, all
> later editions of *Red Cavalry* are based on Babel's *Rasskazy*
> (1936).

Izbrannoe. Moscow: Khudozh. lit-ry, 1966.
Konarmiia, Odesskie rasskazy, p'esy. Letchworth: Bradda Books, 1965.
Izbrannoe. Moscow: Gos. izd-vo khudozh. lit-ry, 1957.
Izbrannoe. Kamerovo: Kamerovskoe knizhoe izd-vo, 1966.
> With a preface by Il'ia Ehrenburg.

Detstvo i drugie rasskazy. Jerusalem: Biblioteka-Aliia, 1979 (2d edition,
1989).
> The only unexpurgated edition. With an essay by Simon
> Markish, "Russko-evreiskaia literatura i Isaak Babel'."

Sochineniia v dvukh tomakh. Moscow: Khudozh. lit-ry, 1990.
> The most complete edition thus far of Babel's works. Includes
> early stories and journalism and his 1920 diary.

Editions in English

Red Cavalry. Translated by N. Helstein. New York: Knopf, 1929.
Collected Stories. Edited and translated by Walter Morison, with an
introduction by Lionel Trilling. New York: New American Library,
1955.
> A revision of the Helstein translation, which abounds in errors
> and is generally an inadequate rendering of Babel's distinctive
> prose. Lionel Trilling's introduction is one of the most frequently
> cited classics.

Lyubka the Cossack and Other Stories. Translated and with an afterword
by Andrew MacAndrew. New York: The New American Library,
1963.
> Corrects some of the errors in Morison but is otherwise not
> remarkably superior to the earlier translation. Rearranges the

stories in a sequence that obscures Babel's thematic organization of the work.

Collected Stories. Translated by David McDuff. New York: Penguin, 1994.

Generally a much more accurate rendering than Morison's. Most of the factual errors pointed out in the text and notes of the present volume have been corrected. Contains helpful historical and geographical notes and a reprint of Trilling's introduction.

1920 Diary. Translated by H. T. Willetts and edited, introduced, and annotated by Carol J. Avins. New Haven, Conn.: Yale University Press, 1995.

Babel's notes on the Polish campaign, many of which he later drew on for the stories of *Red Cavalry.*

Books and Monographs

Included here are books that deal exclusively with *Red Cavalry* or that contain substantial sections on the work.

Belaia, G. A., E. A. Dobrenko, and I. A. Esaulov. *"Konarmiia" Isaaka Babelia.* Moscow: Rossiiskii universitet, 1993.

A general essay by the critic Galina Belaia, followed by a detailed analysis of the structure of the cycle and a piece on "Pan Apolek."

Bloom, Harold, ed. *Isaac Babel.* New York: Chelsea House, 1987.

Reprints of memoirs and scholarly and critical articles on Babel, including several on *Red Cavalry.*

Carden, Patricia. *The Art of Isaac Babel.* Ithaca: Cornell University Press, 1972.

Ehre, Milton. *Isaac Babel.* Boston: Twayne, 1986.

Falen, James. *Isaac Babel: Russian Master of the Short Story.* Knoxville: University of Tennessee, 1974.

Falen's, Ehre's, and Carden's books are all excellent introductions to Babel. Each devotes at least one full chapter to *Red Cavalry.*

Grøngaard, Ragna. *An Investigation of Composition and Theme in Isaak Babel's Literary Cycle Konarmija.* Slavonic Studies 1. Aarhus: Arkona, 1979.

A brief survey of composition and theme.

Hallett, R. *Isaac Babel.* Letchworth: Bradda Books, 1972.

Ingram, F. *Representative Short Story Cycles of the Twentieth Century: Studies in a Literary Genre.* The Hague: Mouton, 1971.

Contains a chapter on *Red Cavalry.*

Luck, C. D. *The Field of Honour: An Analysis of Babel's Na pole chesti*. Birmingham: Birmingham Slavonic Monographs, no. 18, 1987.
Discusses thematic and stylistic links between this cycle of stories and *Red Cavalry*.

Luplow, Carol. *Isaac Babel's Red Cavalry*. Ann Arbor: Ardis, 1982.
Thus far the most extensive general work devoted exclusively to *Red Cavalry*.

Sicher, Efraim. *Style and Structure in the Prose of Isaak Babel*. Columbus: Slavica, 1985.
An excellent study on Babel's style in general, with discussions of numerous passages in *Red Cavalry*. Contains a comprehensive bibliography.

Schreurs, Marc. *Procedures of Montage in Isaak Babel's Red Cavalry*. Studies in Slavic Literature and Poetics 15. Amsterdam: Rodopi, 1989.
A detailed study of the central structural principle of *Red Cavalry*. Contains an illuminating close reading of "Crossing into Poland."

Stora-Sandor, Judith. *Isaac Babel'. L'homme et l'oeuvre*. Paris: Klincksieck, 1968.
The most extensive biography of Babel.

van Baak, J. J. *The Place of Space in Narration: A Semiotic Approach to the Problem of Literary Space. With an Analysis of the Role of Space in I. E. Babel's Konarmiya*. Studies in Slavic Literature and Poetics 3. Amsterdam: Rodopi, 1983.
The theoretical discussion of literary space in the first half of the book is followed by a detailed analysis of space in *Red Cavalry* in which this aspect is linked to the themes and structure of the cycle as a whole.

Articles in Journals and Collections

Andrew, Joe. "Structure and Style in the Short Story: Babel's 'My First Goose.'" *Modern Language Review* 70, no. 2 (1975): 366–79.
———. "'Spoil the Purest of Ladies': Male and Female in Isaac Babel's *Konarmiya*." *Essays in Poetics* 14, no. 8 (1989): 1–27.
A feminist reading of *Red Cavalry*.

Avins, Carol J. "Kinship and Concealment in *Red Cavalry* and Isaac Babel's 1920 Diary." *Slavic Review* 53, no. 3 (Fall 1994): 694–709.
Discusses Babel's relationship to his Jewishness based on the stories and the diary.

Belaia, G. A. "I my uslishali velikoe bezmolvie rubki." See G. A.
Belaia et al. in the "Books and Monographs" section above.

Brown, Edward J. "Isaac Babel: Horror in a Minor Key." In his
Russian Literature since the Revolution, 115–24. New York: Collier,
1963.

Carden, Patricia. "Babel's Two Ivans." *Russian Literature* 15, no. 3
(1984): 299–320.
The entire issue is devoted to Babel.

Danow, David K. "A Poetics of Inversion: The Non-Dialogic Aspect
in Isaac Babel's *Red Cavalry*." *Modern Language Review* 86, no. 4
(1991): 937–53.
Describes the lack of dialogic exchange between the "voices" in
the work as a basic feature of world view.

———. "The Paradox of *Red Cavalry*." *Canadian Slavonic Papers* 36,
nos. 1–2 (March–June 1994): 43–54.
Red Cavalry as a frustrated need for the understanding of
violence. In a Babel centenary issue of the journal.

Davies, Norman. "Izaak Babel's 'Konarmiya' Stories and the
Polish-Soviet War." *Modern Language Review* 67, no. 4 (1972):
845–57.
A historian's attempt to read literature as fact.

Dobrenko, E. A. "Logika tsikla." See G. A. Belaia et al. in the "Books
and Monographs" section above.

Éppel, Asar. "'Opechatki' v izdaniiakh Babelia." *Voprosy literatury* 1
(1995): 92–95.
Included in a round-table discussion of editions of Babel's
works.

Erlich, Victor. "Color and Line: The Art of Isaac Babel." In his
Modernism and Revolution. Cambridge, Mass.: Harvard University
Press, 1994.
Reprint of an article on Babel's style.

Esaulov, I. A. "Eticheskoe i esteticheskoe v rasskaze 'Pan Apolek.'"
See G. A. Belaia et al. in the "Books and Monographs" section
above.

Falchikov, M. "Conflict and Contrast in Isaak Babel's Konarmiya."
Modern Language Review 72, no. 1 (1977): 125–33.
On contrast as the basic thematic and stylistic principle of the
work.

Flaker, Aleksandar. "Babel' i pol'skoe sakral'noe iskusstvo." *Russian
Literature* 22 (1987): 29–38.
Discusses the late baroque Ukranian and Polish folk-inspired

paintings described especially in "Pan Apolek" and "In St.
Valentine's Church."

Friedberg, Maurice. "Yiddish Folklore Motifs in Isaac Babel's
Konarmija." In *American Contributions to the Eighth International
Congress of Slavists, Zagreb-Liubliana, 1979*, 192–203. Columbus:
Slavica Publishers, 1978.

Gereben, Agnes. "Über die Kohäranz einer epischen Gattung:
Spezifische Gattungselemente im Oeuvre von I. Babel insbesondere
im Werk Die Reiterarmee." *Studia Slavica Academiae Scientarum
Hungaricae* 27 (1981): 213–28.

———. "Some Aspects of Narration in the Composition of Cycles of
Short Stories." *Studia Slavica Academiae Hungraricae* 28 (1982):
333–47.

———. "Isaac Babel's Diary and His '*Red Cavalry*.'" *Hungaro-Slavica
1983*. IX. *Internationaler Slavistenkongress, Kiev, 6–13 September
1983*, 55–59. Cologne: Böhau Verlag.

———. "The Writer's Ego in the Composition of Short Stories."
Essays in Poetics 9, no. 1 (1984): 38–77.
On the writer-narrator relationship in *Red Cavalry*.

———. "The Syntactics of Cycles of Short Stories." *Essays in Poetics*
11, no. 1 (1986): 44–75.
On the structure of the cycle, with special attention to the
compositional role of story titles.

Hetenyi, Zsuzsa. "The Visible Idea: Babel's Modelling Imagery."
Canadian Slavonic Papers 36, nos. 1–2 (March–June 1994): 55–68.
On the relationship between images and ideas. In a Babel
centenary issue of the journal.

Hyman, S. "Identities of Isaac Babel." *Hudson Review* 8, no. 4 (1956):
149–52.

Iribarne, Louis. "Babel's *Red Cavalry* as a Baroque Novel."
Contemporary Literature 14, no. 1 (1973): 58–77.
Discusses Babel's use of contrasts, colors, visual exuberance, etc.
as features associated with the Renaissance baroque.

Kheteni [Hetényi], Zhuzha. "Eskadronnaia dama, vozvedennaia v
madonnu. Ambivalentnost; v 'Konarmii' Isaaka Babelia." *Studia
Slavica Academiae Hungraricae* 31 (1985): 161–69.
On images of women in *Red Cavalry*.

———. "Fol'klor'nye elementy v 'Konarmii' Babelia." *Studia Slavica
Academiae Hungraricae* 34 (1988): 237–46.

Khimukhina, N. I. "O zhanrovoi spetsifike 'Konarmii' I. Babelia."
Vestnik Moskovskogo universiteta. Seriia 9, Filologiia 3 (1991): 26–32.

Klotz, Martin B. "Poetry of the Present: Isaac Babel's Red Cavalry."
  Slavic and East European Journal 18, no. 2 (1974): 160–69.
  Analyzes especially "Italian Sunshine."
Kogan, É. "Rabota nad 'Konarmiei' v svete polnoi versii 'planov i
  nabroskov.'" *Voprosy literatury* 1 (1995): 78–87.
  Included in a round-table discussion of editions of Babel's
  works.
Kornblatt, Judith. "Isaac Babel and His Red Cavalry Cossacks." In her
  *The Cossack Hero in Russian Literature: A Study in Cultural
  Mythology.* Madison: University of Wisconsin Press, 1992.
  Argues that the appeal of the image of the Cossack lay in
  its ability to unite the contradictions of the Russian character.
  A chapter on *Red Cavalry* compares Babel to Tolstoi and
  Gogol.
Kovskii, V. "Sud'ba tekstov v kontekste sud'by." *Voprosy literatury* 1
  (1995): 23–78.
  A detailed review of the many editions of Babel's works. Part of
  a round-table discussion of the subject.
Lachmann, R. "Notizen zu I. Babels 'Perechod čerez Zbruč.'" In
  Vozm'i na radost': To Honour Jeanne van der Eng-Leidmeier, 183–92.
  Amsterdam: Rodolpi, 1980.
  On "Crossing into Poland."
Lee, Alice. "Epiphany in Babel's Red Cavalry." *Russian Literature
  Triquarterly* 2 (1972): 249–60.
Leiderman, N. "I Ia khochu internatsional dobrykh liudei."
  Literaturnoe obozrenie 10 (1991): 11–18.
  A re-evaluation of Babel's position on the Revolution which
  stresses his humanist values.
Leiter, L. "A Reading of Isaac Babel's 'Crossing into Poland.'" *Studies
  in Short Fiction* 3, no. 2 (1966): 199–206.
Livshits, L. "Materialy k tvorcheskoi biografii I. Babelia." *Voprosy
  literatury* 4 (1964): 110–34.
Lowe, David. "A Generic Approach to Babel's Red Cavalry." *Modern
  Fiction Studies* 28, no. 1 (1982): 69–78.
  Discusses links between *Red Cavalry* and the Renaissance
  novella.
Marder, H. "The Revolutionary Art of Babel'." *Novel* 7 (1973–74):
  54–61.
Masing-Delic, Irene. "Bright Hopes and Dark Insights: Vision and
  Cognition in Babel's Red Cavalry." In Michael S. Flier and Robert
  E. Hughes, eds., *For SK: In Celebration of the Life and Career of*

Simon Karlinsky, 199–210. Berkeley: Berkeley Slavic Specialties, 1994.

Merkin, G. S. "S. Budennyi i I. Babel (k istorii polemiki)." *Filologicheskie nauki* 4 (1990): 97–102.

Mihailovich, Vasa. "Assessments of Isaac Babel." *Papers on Language and Literature* 9, no. 3 (Summer 1973): 323–42.
  Contains extensive bibliography.

Murphy, A. B. "The Style of Isaak Babel'." *Slavonic and East European Review* 44 (1966): 361–80.

Nakhimovsky, Alice Stone. "Isaac Babel." In her *Russian-Jewish Literature and Identity: Jabotinsky, Babel, Grossman, Galich, Roziner, Markish*, 70–107. Baltimore: The Johns Hopkins University Press, 1992.
  Sets Babel's Jewish identity in the broader context of twentieth-century Russian-Jewish literature.

Nilsson, Nils Åke. "Isaak Babel's 'Perechod čerez Zbruč.'" *Scando-Slavica* 23 (1977): 63–71.
  On "Crossing into Poland."

Poggioli, Renato. "Isaac Babel in Retrospect." In his *The Phoenix and the Spider*. Cambridge: Harvard University Press, 1957.
  An early but still much cited overview of Babel.

Povartsov, Sergei. "Isaak Babel': portret na fone Lubianki." *Voprosy literatury* 3 (1995): 21–72.
  On Babel's early involvement with the Cheka, his plans for a novel on the subject, and his arrest and execution.

Reid, Alan. "Isaak Babel's *Konarmiia*: Meanings and Endings." *Canadian Slavonic Papers* 33, no. 2 (June 1991): 139–50.
  Discusses especially "The Rebbe's Son" and "Argamak."

Ross, R. "The Unity of Babel's Konarmija." *South Central Bulletin* 41, no. 4 (1981): 114–19.

Sarnov, Benedikt. "Kak opredelit' avtorskuiu voliu." *Voprosy literatury* 1 (1995): 87–92.
  Lists the many deletions and revisions in later editions of *Red Cavalry*. Part of a round-table discussion on editions of Babel's works.

Schreurs, Marc. "Montage as a Constructing Principle in Cinematic and Narrative Art: Éjzenštejn and Babel'." *Russian Literature* 19, no. 2 (1986): 193–254.

———. "Two Forms of Montage in Babel's *Konarmija*." *Russian Literature* 21 (1987): 243–92.
  Discusses inner stories and digressions as montage techniques.

———. "Intertextual Montage in Babel's *Konarmija*." In *Dutch Contributions to the Tenth International Congress of Slavists, Sofia, September 14–22, 1988*, 277–307. Amsterdam: Rodopi, 1988.

All three of Schreurs's articles develop chapters in his book (see above).

Shcheglov, Yuri K. "Some Themes and Archetypes in Babel's *Red Cavalry*." *Slavic Review* 53, no. 3 (Fall 1994): 653–70.

An analysis of archetypal motifs in "My First Goose."

Sicher, Efraim. "The Duality of the Alienated Jewish Narrator in Modern Jewish Literature: An Analysis of Semiotic Modelling in the Prose of Isaak Babel." *Proceedings of the Eighth World Congress of Jewish Studies*, vol. 3, 129–34. Jerusalem: World Union of Jewish Studies, 1982.

———. "Isaac Babel's Jewish Roots." *Jewish Quarterly* 25 (1977–78): 25–27.

———. "Art as Metaphor. Epiphany and Aesthetic Statement: The Short Stories of Isaak Babel." *Modern Language Review* 77, no. 2 (1982): 387–96.

On Babel's stories as comments on the nature of art and reality.

———. "Isaak Babel: Voyeur of the Short Story." *Stand* 23, no. 2 (1982): 54–58.

———. "The Road to a Red Calvary: Myth and Mythology in the Works of Isaac Babel of the 1920s." *Slavonic and East European Review* 60, no. 4 (1982): 528–46.

———. "The Jew on Horseback: On the Question of Isaak Babel's Place in Soviet Jewish Literature." *Soviet Jewish Affairs* 13, no. 1 (1984): 37–50.

———. "The Jewishness of Babel." In Jack Miller, ed., *Jews in Soviet Culture*, 167–82. New Brunswick, N.J.: Transaction Books, 1984.

———. "The 'Jewish Cossack': Isaac Babel in the First Red Cavalry." In Jonathan Frankel, ed., *Studies in Contemporary Jewry*. Vol. 4: *The Jews and the European Crisis, 1914–21*, 113–34. New York: Oxford University Press, 1988.

Analyzes Babel's attitude toward the Jews, based largely on the 1920 diary. Also contains translations of two of Babel's articles in *The Red Cavalryman*.

Sinyavsky, Andrey. "Isaac Babel." In Edward J. Brown, ed., *Major Soviet Writers: Essays in Criticism*, 301–9. New York: Oxford University Press, 1973.

Spektor, U. "Molodoi Babel." *Voprosy literatury* 7 (1982): 278–81.

Babel's early life, based on archival materials.

Stine, Peter. "Isaac Babel and Violence." *Modern Fiction Studies* 30, no. 2 (1984): 237–55.

van Baak, J. J. "The Function of Nature and Space in *Konarmiia* by I. E. Babel." In *Dutch Contributions to the Eighth International Congress of Slavists, Zagreb-Liubliana*. Amsterdam: Benjamins, 1979.

———. "Story and Cycle: Babel's 'Poceluj' and Konarmija." *Russian Literature* 15, no. 3 (1984): 321–46.

On a story ("The Kiss") related to *Red Cavalry* but never included in the collection.

———. "Zur literarischen Physiologie des modernen mythischen Helden. Am Beispiel der Kosaken in Babel's *Konarmija*." *Wiener Slawistischer Almanach*. Sonderband 20 (1987) ("Mythos in der slawischen Moderne"), 349–69.

Discusses Babel's Cossacks in the context of the mythicizing and primitivist components of modernist antirealism.

———. "Isaak Babel's 'Cemetery at Kozin.'" *Canadian Slavonic Papers* 36, nos. 1–2 (March–June 1994): 69–87.

A structural and semantic-semiotic analysis. In a Babel centenary issue of the journal.

van der Eng, Jan. "The Pointed Conclusion as Story Finale and Cyclic Element in *Red Cavalry*." In Benjamin Stolz, I. R. Titunik, and Lubomir Dolezel, eds., *Language and Literary Theory*. Ann Arbor: University of Michigan Press, 1984.

———. "Babel's Short Story 'Zamost'e'." In J. J. van Baak, ed., *Signs of Friendship: To Honour A.G.F. van Holk*. Amsterdam: Rodopi, 1984.

———. "Types of Inner Tales in *Red Cavalry*." In Peter Alberg Jensen, ed., *Text and Context: Essays to Honor Nils Åke Nilsson*, 128–38. Stockholm: Almqvist & Wiksell, 1987.

Examines various kinds of embedded narratives in the work.

———. "Komplizierung der Thematik durch dem Mythos." *Wiener Slawistischer Almanach*. Sonderband 20 (1987) ("Mythos in der slawischen Moderne"), 327–48.

Defines the thematic essence of the work as a clash between messianic Hasidism and Communism.

———. "*Red Cavalry*: A Novel of Stories." *Russian Literature* 33 (1993): 249–64.

Discusses devices that impart a novel-like continuity to the cycle.

Williams, Gareth. "Two Leitmotifs in Babel's *Konarmija*." *Die Welt der Slaven* 17, no. 2 (1972): 279–98.

On the sun and the moon as recurring motifs.

————. "The Rhetoric of Revolution in Babel's *Konarmija.*" *Russian Literature* 15, no. 3 (1984): 279–98.

Stresses Babel's commitment to the Revolution. The entire issue is devoted to Babel.

Young, Richard. "Theme in Fictional Literature: A Way into Complexity." *Language and Style* 13, no. 3 (1980): 61–71.

On the narrative structure of "Crossing into Poland."

Contributors

Milton Ehre is professor of Russian literature at the University of Chicago. He is the author of *Isaac Babel*.

Carol Luplow Levy is the author of *Isaac Babel's Red Cavalry* and articles on Babel's other works.

Charles Rougle is associate professor of Russian literature and chair of the Department of Germanic and Slavic Languages and Literatures at the State University of New York at Albany. He is the author of "Art and the Artist in Babel's 'Guy de Maupassant.'"

Victor Terras is professor emeritus of Slavic and comparative literature at Brown University. He is the author of numerous monographs on Russian writers and the editor of *Handbook of Russian Literature*.

.